Rescue

2nd Edition

A Novel

By Walter A. Campbell

About the Author

Walter A. Campbell was born in March of 1943, in Jersey City, NJ during World War II while his dad, Walter Sr. was serving in the United States Marine Corp. Walter was one of five children. Several years after the war the family moved to suburban New Jersey where he lived out his youth. He attended Union Collage and following his first wife, Claire's advice took a job with an upstart petroleum company. The company and his career grew, and he retired after 41 years of service, or as Walt jokingly refers to his tenure as 82 six-month probationary periods. His career took him to locations in the United States and the Caribbean, where he held management positions in accounting, finance, operations, and fire service where he rose to the rank of Fire Chief and then Incident Commander.

He also served as Treasurer for a K -12 private school and two municipal economic development boards.

Currently, Walter and his wife Carol spend most of their time in Florida with summers in New Jersey.

Walter's hobbies include painting and golf. Rescue is his first attempt at writing a novel.

*"How big is the universe? The end of counting, times the end of counting!"**

Jersey City street expression, circa1950

Acknowledgements

The writing and publishing of this story would not have been possible without my sister Patrica Staley's grammatical and technical assistance; to Diane McKeever, for her book layout and publishing assistance and last but certainly not least, my wife Carol for her patience and understanding as I whiled away the hours on my computer researching and creating this story.

 ## *2ⁿᵈ Edition - Author Note*

This novel was first published as a narrative focusing on an astronaut rescue from the International Space Station. Starting with Chapter 36, page 197, this 2ⁿᵈ edition adds events arising from that rescue.

Casey Publishing Company LLC

Naples, Florida

Copyright 2025 © by Walter A. Campbell
ISBN 979-8-9911715-2-6
Cover Design – Diane McKeever

Contact: caseypublishing@myyahoo.com

Dedication

This book is dedicated to Ann Maloch, a native of northeastern Pennsylvania and my secretary for well over a decade when I worked in the Caribbean. Ann took my raw business writings and made them into correspondences that were professional, legible, and decipherable. I wish she was still with us to read this book. Thank you, Ann!

Forward

Since man started to walk the face of Earth, he has wondered about the possible existence of beings other than himself. He first explored his own domain, his local. As he became more mobile, he started to explore beyond his horizon, then his continent, and then beyond his seas and oceans. And he found other people like himself.

But until recently, there was one place that he could not go and that was to the sky, the moon and stars and the planets, a place he called Space. Even now this is a place that he knows very little about.

This book tells the story of how his first meeting with people from beyond his planet might take place.

It also reflects on how he has evolved as an Earthling and how he has treated his fellow man.

Author's Note: This book contains facts regarding our plant and our Galaxy," The Milky Way". The author has made a concerted effort to make certain these facts are as true and correct as possible.

Table of Contents

ABOARD INTERNATIONAL SPACE STATION (ISS) ----------------- 1

HOUSTON, TEXAS --10

SPACE --13

ROUTINE--22

ALERT --25

THE LUNCHEON --30

ISS HISTORY--34

EVACUATION PLANNING ------------------------------------38

LEAK ---45

SHUTTLE IS FOUND---54

CLOUD CHANGE--57

THE LAUNCH --63

SAFE HAVEN --67

RAINDROPS ---81

THE HOME FRONT, HOUSTON ------------------------------------87

SEVERED --89

RESCUE---97

THE WORLD OF THE GRACIANS-------------------------------- 101

LRGEV167 --- 106

BACK ON EARTH --- 110

HOMEWARD BOUND -------------------------------------- 112

THE PHONE CALL -- 121

LANDING IN HOUSTON ------------------------------------ 128

MEETING THE ALIENS ------------------------------------ 134

REUNION -- 139

EXTRA, EXTRA, READ ALL ABOUT IT! -------------------------- 142

RECOVERY -- 148

LRGEV167 PROBLEM ------------------------------------- 150

FUEL PROCESSING – FRANCE------------------------------- 158

CERN--- 161

ON TO GERMANY --------------------------------------- 165

DEPARTURE --- 167

CALL FROM THE CENTER --- 169

THE PLAN--- 184

THE SPEECH -- 190

REACTION AND FOLLOW THROUGH---------------------------- 194

THE U N SPEECH + 3 YEARS ------------------------------------- 197

GRACIAN UPDATE --- 203

THE ASTRONAUTS – LIFE AFTER THE RESCUE ---------------- 205

WHAT EARTHLINGS ARE THINKING----------------------------- 211

THE GRACIANS PLAN OF ACTION ------------------------------ 221

THE CLOCK IS TICKING --- 235

THE MEDIA WAKES UP -- 237

PLANET GRACE ARRIVES -- 241

HAZARDS AND DANGERS IN SPACE ---------------------------- 244

"A DAY" IS ALMOST HERE-- 250

ONE WEEK TO GO -- 253

THE GO AHEAD CALL-- 255

PEEK–A-BOO --- 259

"A" DAY AND THE MORNING AFTER ----------------------------- 262

JUST WHEN YOU THOUGHT IT WAS SAFE ---------------------- 264

RUMBLINGS --- 270

ARMAGEDDON -- 276

ALL CLEAR --- 278

AFTERMATH --- 282

Chapter 1

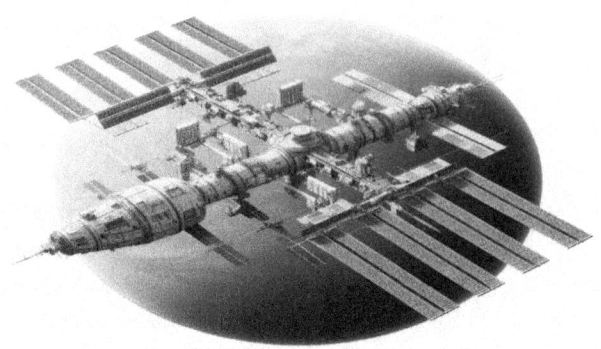

Aboard International Space Station (ISS)

It is mid-January. At 5:45 AM the alarm on U.S. Air Force
Captain Francis (Frank) Hammel's wristwatch has
awakened him from a normal, restful sleep. But where, and
how, he sleeps is anything but normal because Frank
Hammel is one of three astronauts currently occupying the
International Space Station (ISS). He sleeps in a vertical
position tethered to his personal space Compartment.
Captain Hammel is the current Station Commander. Each
Morning at 6:00 AM, he receives a wakeup call from NASA's
Mission Control Center in Houston, Texas. Captain Hammel
likes to be awake when the call comes in. The station is

currently orbiting the Earth at an altitude between 230 to 290 miles in a near circular orbit. This route takes the station over approximately 80% of the earth's population. The ISS is expected to remain in orbit until 2030. At that point, the station will have reached its useful service life and per agreement with the eighteen ISS partners, the station will be taken out of service and destroyed. Their agreed plan for ending the life of the station calls for an orbit adjustment, causing it to enter and burn up as it speeds through the Earth's upper atmosphere. This is a very unceremonious end to a gallant partner that played a key role in space exploration for the past several decades.

Wake-ups, and for that matter, sleeping on the ISS are usually routine, however the lack of gravity alters the way most things are done. The lavatory stop involves the use of a high-tech commode equipped with a vacuum pump, automatic brushes, and foot stirrups. Body washing and teeth brushing are also different with the use of liquid tight containers for washing and rinsing. Eating meals is also different due to the lack of gravity. Food can be chilled or heated but most of it must remain in liquid tight containers. Sandwiches are the exception, they can be made using pita bread, but the ingredients' containers must be secured otherwise they will float away. The crew, which can number up to six, usually eat breakfast and dinner together. This allows for discussion of their work and daily activities. Subjects typically discussed may include experiments, maintenance tasks, communicating with mission control and space observations.

Another important activity is daily exercise. The lack of gravity has an adverse effect on fitness and muscle tone. To combat this deterioration, each crew member exercises about 2 ½ hours per day. The station does have several pieces of exercise equipment on board for this purpose.

The station has accommodation for seven crew members. Currently, there are three crew members on board. They are all Americans. A French crew member and two Japanese Astronauts have recently rotated back to earth aboard a cargo flight and their replacements, two Russian Cosmonauts have not yet arrived back on board.

Captain Hammel is preparing for his radio report to Mission Control in Houston.

"Mission Control to ISS, over"

"Good morning, Mission Control. This is Commander Frank Hammel of the International Space Station. All is well up here and we have no serious issues or concerns to report. After this report, I will be sending a list of food supplies and consumables to add to the Next Supply Flight list. I will also be sending a list of supplies that are required for some minor maintenance work. This work will be discussed and approved by NASA engineers before any of it proceeds. That's it from my end, do you have anything for us? "

"Captain, this is Doug Rayson from the Mission Control group. Everything looks good in our part of the Galaxy. We have had something pop up on our radio telescope system. I believe it is too far out for you to pick it up with your optical telescope or radar. As best we can determine it appears to be an amorphous shape. We are not even sure whether it's gas or solid. It may be a meteor type mass. We just don't know. As I said, it's very far away and we're not even sure if it's travelling in our direction. We will continue our observation and let you know if anything changes. We are also expecting some Solar Flare activity today which may affect communications later on, but it is nothing out of the ordinary. Thank you, Captain Hammel."

One of the perils facing the ISS is a meteor or an asteroid strike. Even a small meteor shower can cause significant harm to the station. "Space Junk", or debris, i.e. abandoned satellites, burned-out rocket stages, space probes, communication or spy satellites that have fallen out of their orbit are all threats to the ISS. Because of these perils, which are uncontrollable, NASA employs an entire department, The ISS Surveillance Group, whose sole task is to watch for any items that could threaten the life and safety of the ISS. They do this 24 hours a day, 7 days a week. The European Space Agency, ESA, estimates that there are more than 29,000 pieces of space debris with a size greater than 4 inches in earth's orbit at the present time. The ISS is equipped with optical and radio telescopes, radar, and sonar to aid in this surveillance, but this is not done on a 24/7 basis. This equipment is also used for celestial navigation checks and to support the station's scientific experiments.

The ISS does have thrusters that help keep it in the proper orbit, but they are not meant, nor can they move the station, out of the way of any approaching object.

If a collision with any type of harmful space object was inevitable all station personnel would be evacuated back to earth. This has never happened. NASA does have detailed evacuation plans in place, and they are reviewed on a regular basis. Evacuation drills are also conducted frequently.

Another space phenomenon to deal with are solar flares. These flares are sudden explosions of energy that occur in the sun's atmosphere. They are caused by the reorganization of magnetic field lines near sunspots. Solar flares release a great deal of energy into space, including electromagnetic radiation and charged particles. If a solar flare is very intense, the radiation it releases can interfere with radio wave transmissions on Earth. Solar Flares are a nuisance not a threat. Depending on their intensity they can temporarily interrupt communications between Earth and the ISS.

The second crew member aboard ISS is Gloria Fan, aged 29. Ms. Fan was born and raised in Southern California. Her parents migrated from Taipei, Taiwan in the 1980's. She attended the University of California, Davis where she earned an undergraduate degree in biology and a master's degree in environmental science. Gloria then received a fellowship from the University of Nebraska where she earned a PhD in Micro-Biotic Farming. Gloria is currently Co-Chair of NASA's agricultural research team. This is her third trip to the ISS. On this trip she is continuing her work on common agricultural plant propagation without the help of birds or bees. She calls it "insemination without the fun". Gloria has also participated in a NASA study on the effects of weightlessness on the female side of human reproduction.

"Captain Hammel, this is Jethro Teal of NASA's agricultural team. Is Ms. Fan available for a quick conversation?"

"Yes, and you should be quick because NASA is predicting some solar flare interference which may affect this call. We are expecting to arrive at the area of interference in about 12 to 15 minutes."

"Thank you, Captain."

"Hello, Jethro this is Gloria, I understand you had a question."

"Yes. My question is about plant insemination. I see that you have done some work in this area.

"Gloria, "Yes, I have."

Jethro, "Have you experimented with any gene or DNA alteration? I am particularly interested in altered seeds that have been inseminated. "Gloria, "Yes, I have on a limited basis. The results have ranged from zero germination to deformed, abnormal, and normal seed and growth. My testing is far from complete, and much more work is needed.

We should also talk about something else I stumbled upon while doing this research. I call it Micro-Oxygen Plant Infusion (MOPI). I have filed a research notice on this subject. And like the plant DNA alteration project, a lot more work is required before an actual research paper can be developed. It works like this: seed pods are placed in an airtight container. The oxygen content inside the container is then adjusted from the normal 14% to a level of 40%. This change in oxygen percentage has an amazing positive effect on seed and plant growth. Right now, I have a full plate of project experiments to do up here so I do not know when I will get back to this work. Let me give it more thought (static) and I will get (static) back to you (static) Gloria (static-static) over and out (static-static-static)".

Jethro Teal to NASA Communications. "It looks like a solar flare just temporarily ended my conversation with ISS".

The third member of the crew is Rakib Rajbir, age 38. Rakib is originally from Bhopal, India. He attended the Indian Institute of Technologies, Madras which is one of India's most prestigious technical colleges. He graduated 8th in his undergraduate class of 3,600 students and received a bachelor's degree in electrical engineering. He then went on to earn a master's degree in Robotic Science and then studied Aeronautical Engineering with an emphasis on Aerospace Flight Theory. This course of study earned him a PhD in Aerospace Science. Rakib is considered an expert in this field. He was recruited directly out of college by NASA and has worked for them ever since. He returned to India to select a bride. He and his wife Asha have two children, a girl Siri age 13 and a son Sandeep age 11.

Currently, Rakib is head of a NASA team who are studying the feasibility of extending the remaining ISS service life beyond its current 30-year period which expires in 2030. Rakib and his team have developed some very ambitious plans, and they carry a high price tag. He sees the successful completion of this assignment as a means of furthering his NASA ambitions and career. As part of the project, Rakib insists that he needs to complete an external inspection (spacewalk) of the ISS before he can finish his work. NASA believes the walk is not necessary as there is a mountain of ISS information that already exists to support his study. Further, and aside from the obvious risks, some higher ups at NASA believe that Rakib's request for an external ISS inspection is nothing more than a ploy to experience a spacewalk. This is a current point of contention between NASA and Mr. Rajbir.

With the morning NASA Communication ended, Captain Hammel, Gloria Fan and Rakib Rajbir begin their daily work routines.

Under normal circumstances the ISS crew complement would number about six. However, as mentioned, the replacements for the two Japanese astronauts have not yet arrived back at ISS. Russia was supposed to supply the replacements and the transportation to the station, but they claimed technical issues related to their Soyuz spacecraft have delayed the flight. NASA believes that there is more to the delay, but they have no proof.

Chapter 2

Houston, Texas

Captain Hammel's wife Patrica, Patty to her friends, has gotten her two children off to school and is getting ready to attend a luncheon given by Ashly Sosa, wife of NASA director Ernesto Sosa. Ashly holds a luncheon once a month for a handful of wives of NASA higher ups. She also includes the wives of any astronauts who are currently aboard the ISS. Ashly is a kind, thoughtful and very engaging person who makes good use of her position in the NASA society hierarchy.

Patty has known Frank Hammel since high school in Albuquerque, New Mexico. But their friendship was interrupted when they went off to different colleges. Frank was accepted and attended the Air Force Academy in Colorado Springs. Patty attended New Mexico State's School of Medicine where she received her Registered Nurses Degree. She is currently a Supervisor of Operating Room Nurses at Houston Methodist Hospital in Clear Lake. The Hammels live in Melody Estates, a subdivision of Houston and a favorite residence for NASA workers.

Patty is awaiting a pickup by Asha Rajbir who lives close by in the more upscale subdivision of Imperial Estates. After arriving in America as the newlywed wife of Rakib, Asha attended Rice University where she received a degree in Aeronautical Engineering. She currently works from home as an Air Safety Engineer for the Federal Aviation Authority. Ironically, Asha does not like to fly. Her two children attend private schools.

The two wives get along well, and today's discussion starts out about when their husbands will arrive back on earth. Their current schedule calls for a return in mid-May. That will make their stay aboard ISS about 8 months long.

"119 days to go and the guys will be home!" Says Patty. "I am so looking forward to it. Frank and I decided that after his return, including transitional medical exams and technical debriefings, school will be out for this summer season so we will take the kids on a four-week tour of the west including California. We want to be sure to see the Grand Canyon, Death Valley, some of the other desert parks and the Pacific Coast highway. We both love the beach, so San Diego is also on our radar. I am working on an itinerary right now and once I get it set, I'll make the reservations and off we will go! I think we will stop for two or three days at each place. It should be fun."

Asha, "We didn't make any solid plans, but we would like to go to Disney World in Orlando. We have been to the park in

California, and we loved it, but they say Disney Orlando is even better. We may even stay in Tomorrow Land but maybe not because by then Rakib may have had his fill outer space stuff for a while! But I will say that after 240 days away it will be good to see him again."

Asha, "Well here we are, Tung Shing House. I love Asian food, and this restaurant has at least 2 dishes on the menu that are seasoned with Curry, so here goes my diet!"

Chapter 3

Space

Appointing the on-board commander of the ISS depends upon who is on board. Most times a military person with an officer's rank is on board so the job usually goes to that person. However, a civilian can also be appointed and if so that person usually has some degree of managerial education or experience.

At this point in time, U.S. Air Force Captain Francis (Frank) Hammel is the appointed commander. In this capacity, Captain Hammel has a number of duties and responsibilities he is expected to perform each day. He is the official point of contact for the ISS. He also serves as the station's ambassador, crew arbitrator, decision maker/approver and overall head-guy-in-charge. Each crew member also has a number of duty assignments such as housekeeping, sanitary chores, and repairs and maintenance work. There are no housekeepers, cooks, or maintenance personnel aboard ISS. All tasks required to keep the station "shipshape" fall to captain and crew. And it is up to Commander Hammel to see these tasks are done in a proper and timely manner.

Captain Hammel will start his day today by surveying the station to ensure that its operational, health, and safety aspects are all up to standard. Certain scheduled mechanical, electrical, and electronic checks will be carried out by both the captain and members of the crew. The objective is to discover potential problems and fix them before they become major issues. NASA ISS support in Houston plays a major support role in this endeavor.

With the day's review of the station complete, Captain Hammel has decided to follow up NASA's report of the unknown item which they have spotted off in the very far distance from earth and the ISS. He does not expect to see much, figuring that if NASA, with their more powerful electronic and optical telescopes and listening devices can't classify it then he probably won't do any better. However, he does have the advantage of clearer views due to less light and particle pollution which are present when peering through Earth's atmosphere. Using the coordinates supplied by NASA and ISS's optical telescope Captain Hammel peers through space. He sees some planets and the millions of stars and other objects that make up the universe. But there is no sign of anything that would give cause for concern. As he looks through the telescope, he is once again reminded of the vastness of space and Earth's place in it.

Our place in the Universe is known as the Milky Way Galaxy. The term Milky Way is a translation of the Latin phrase, "via lacteal". It contains our Solar System including Earth, 7 other plants and our Sun. The name Milky Way describes the galaxy's appearance from Earth: an irregular luminous, hazy band of light seen in the sky. The band is formed from stars and gas clouds that stretch across the entire galaxy.

Galileo first observed the band of light with his telescope in 1610. Until the early 1920s, most astronomers thought that the Milky Way contained all the stars in the Universe. Following the Big Bang theory debate of the 1920's between the astronomers Harlow Shapley and Heber Curtis, and observations by Edwin Hubble it was determined that the Milky Way is just one of many galaxies.

The Galaxy, as it is referred to by the astronomical community, is a large spiral system consisting of several hundred billion stars. Earth lies well within its parameters. A thick layer of interstellar dust obscures much of the Galaxy from scrutiny by optical telescopes. Astronomers have determined its large-scale structure with the aid of radio and infrared telescopes, which can detect the forms of radiation that penetrate the obscuring matter.

The Galaxy is made up of several components; singular or double stars (suns) are the largest. They also exist as conspicuous groups and clusters that contain tens of thousands of members.

The next largest group is a collection of large, bright, diffused gaseous clouds called planet nebulae. These nebulae resemble planetary disks when viewed through a telescope. They represent a stage at the end of their stellar life cycle rather than one at the beginning. There are more than 1,000 known planetary nebulae in the Galaxy, but more might be overlooked because of obscuration in the Milky Way region.

Another type of nebulous object found in the Galaxy is a supernova. These are remnants of gases blown out from exploding stars.

The first reliable measurement of the Galaxy's size was made in 1917 by American astronomer Harlow Shapley. He found that, instead of a relatively small system with the Sun near its center, as had previously been thought, the Galaxy is immense, with the Sun nearer the edge. Assuming that the globular clusters outlined the Galaxy, he determined that it has a diameter of about 100,000 light-years and that the Sun lies about 30,000 light-years from the center. His values have held up remarkably well over the years. Current scientific calculations confirm Shapley's diameter measurement and put the Sun 5,000 light years closer to the center of the Galaxy.

A Light Year is the distance light will travel in one year. Light travels at 186,000 miles per second. That is the Equivalent of traveling equatorially around the earth 7 ½ times in one second or 671 million miles per hour; 16.1 billion miles per day or 5.9 trillion miles per year. Stated another way, if an object is 10 light years from earth it is 59 trillion miles away and the sight of it took ten years to get here.

When we use powerful telescopes to look at distant objects in space, we are actually looking back in time. How can this be? Light travels extremely fast, but objects in space are so far away that it takes a lot of time for their light to reach us. The farther away an object is, the farther in the past we see it.

Our Sun is the closest star to us, about 93 million miles away. So, the Sun's light takes about 8.3 minutes to reach us. This means that we always see the Sun as it was about 8.3 minutes ago. The next closest star to us is about 4.3 light-years away. When we see this star today, we are seeing it as it was 4.3 years ago. All the other stars we see are farther, some thousands of light years away.

The Milky Way Galaxy's structure and shape is fairly typical of a large spiral system. It has six separate parts: (1) a nucleus, (2) a central bulge, (3) a disk (4) spiral arms, (5) a spherical component, and (6) a massive halo. Some of these components blend into each other.

The most interesting and remarkable part of the Galaxy's structure is the nucleus and its accompanying accretion disk. Located at the very center of the Galaxy, the nucleus is, in all likelihood, a massive black hole surrounded by an accretion disk of high-temperature gas. Neither this central object nor any of the material immediately around it can be observed at optical wavelengths because of the thick screen of intervening dust in the Milky Way. The object, however, is readily detectable at radio wavelengths and has been dubbed Sagittarius A by radio astronomers. This galactic nucleus is the site of a wide range of activity apparently powered by the black hole itself. Infrared radiation and X-rays are emitted from the area, and rapidly moving gas clouds can be observed. Data strongly indicates that material is being pulled into the black hole from outside the nucleus region. Rotation measurements of the disk and the orbital motions of stars indicate that the black hole has a mass 4.3 million times that of the Sun!

The Milky Way moves through space at a velocity of about 1.2 million miles per hour. The stars, gas and dust of the Milky Way all orbit the center at a rate of about 500,000 miles per hour. This constant rate for all stars at different distances from the core implies the existence of a shell of dark matter surrounding our galaxy.

Our galaxy will collide with the adjacent Andromeda Galaxy in about 5 billion years. No one knows for sure what will happen.

In summary, The Milky Way began as a series of dense regions in the early universe not long after the Big Bang. The first stars to form were in globular clusters and they still exist. It has grown by merging with other galaxies. It is currently acquiring stars from a small galaxy called the Sagittarius Dwarf Spheroidal, as well as gobbling up material from the Magellanic Clouds.

Our Milky Way is a part of the Physical Universe which is defined as all of space and time and their contents. It is collectively referred to as Spacetime. Such contents comprise all of energy in its various forms, including electromagnetic radiation and matter, and therefore includes planets, moons, stars, galaxies, and other contents of intergalactic space. The universe also includes the physical laws that influence energy and matter, such as conservation laws, classical mechanics, and relativity.

The universe is often defined as "the totality of existence", or everything that exists, everything that has existed, and everything that will exist. In fact, some philosophers and scientists support the inclusion of ideas and abstract concepts, such as mathematics and logic, in their definition of the universe. The word universe may also refer to concepts such as the cosmos, the world, and nature.

The word universe comes from the French word univers, which in turn originated from the Latin word universum.

Current scientific thinking has the universe being "born" out of the rapid expansion from an initial state of extremely high density and unimaginably hot temperature. This event is referred to as the Big Bang. It took place when the universe was just, a hundredth of a billionth of a trillionth of a trillionth of a second in age. The Big Bang theory is a cosmological model of the observable universe from the earliest known periods through its subsequent large-scale evolution. The theory was developed during the 1920's. For several decades, the scientific community was divided between supporters of the Big Bang and the rival Steady-State model, but a wide range of empirical evidence has strongly favored the Big Bang, which is now universally accepted.

The Big Bang is not an explosion of matter moving outward to fill an empty universe because space itself expands with time everywhere and increases the physical distances between co-moving points. In other words, the Big Bang is not an expsion in space, but rather an expansion of space.

People describe the Universe as huge, enormous, massive, vast, gargantuan, colossal, or just plain, big. However, these words are all understatements. There may not be a single word that actually describe its size other than perhaps, infinite.

Another reason the size of the universe is difficult, if not impossible, to define is because of the general theory of relativity, which in part states that far regions of the universe may never interact with closer areas even in the lifetime of the universe due to the finite speed of light vs. the ongoing expansion of space. Even if the universe were to exist forever, a laser beam of light or a radio signal sent from Earth may never reach some outer regions of space because the universe is believed to be expanding faster than light can traverse it. We simply do not know the limits of the universe, if indeed there are limits!

Distant regions of space are assumed to exist and to be part of reality as much as we are, even though we can never interact with them. The spatial region that we can affect and be affected by is the observable universe. The observable universe depends on the location of the observer. By traveling, an observer can encounter a greater region of spacetime than an observer who remains still. Nevertheless, even the most rapid traveler will not be able to interact with all of space. Typically, the observable universe is taken to mean the portion of the universe that is observable from our vantage point in the Milky Way.

All right, so we cannot measure the size of the Universe. But do we know how old it is? A number of calculations and models have been developed in an attempt to answer this question. A consensus put forth by the astro–scientific community puts the estimated age of the Universe at 13.8 billion years, give or take a quarter billion but there are a lot of assumptions that go along with this, so it is far from exact. Still, that is a lot of years.

Narratives about other components, elements, and features of the Milky Way Galaxy fill volumes. Capt. Hammel will stop his reflecting here for he has once again reminded himself just how infinite the universe really is.

Chapter 4

Routine

Another week has passed aboard the ISS and by all accounts the days have gone by quite normally. It is Monday evening and the three crew members have gathered for the evening meal. Food available on the ISS includes, frozen vegetables and desserts, refrigerated food, fruit, dairy products, sealed pouches of American food, canned Russian food, like lamb with vegetables or chicken with rice, brownies and fruit that can be eaten in their natural forms, and foods that require adding water, such as macaroni and cheese or spaghetti. An oven is provided in the space station to heat foods to the proper temperature. Astronauts totally agree on two things when it comes to dining; "No one goes to space for the food, but the views are amazing" and "hot sauce makes everything taste better!" Before the first flights into space, scientists weren't even sure if swallowing in zero gravity was possible.

Capt. Hammel, "Gloria, what's that you're eating?

Gloria, "This is the latest result of one of my research projects, I call it a space cheeseburger, it consists of a microwaved beef patty, cheese, tomato paste, and Russian mustard all wrapped in a tortilla."

Capt. Hammel, "how does it taste?"

Gloria, "Pass the hot sauce."

Rakib, "I am dining on a squeeze tube special of chicken and rice with a heavy dose of curry sauce. I think curried chicken and rice is the unofficial national dinner of India!"

"How about you captain?"

"I'm not that hungry, so I went with peanut butter and jelly on a Pita. I'll follow this up with tea and a brownie for dessert."

"Seriously, Gloria, how are your agriculture experiments going?"

Gloria, "They're growing quite well. My cherry tomato patch is already yielding fruit. It's interesting to see tomatoes float upward and still be attached to the vine. And the fruit itself is just a perfect color and shape and there's no bruising or insect damage. I believe we're proving that fruits and vegetables can be grown in space. I believe we can also grow things on other planets provided shelters were set up to ward off the harsh environmental conditions."

Capt. Hammel, "I heard you mention doing some type of experiment with oxygen. I think you called it oxygen infusion or something like that. Does that work show any promise?"

Gloria, "I think it may but a lot more testing and experimenting needs to be done and also finding the time to do it."

Capt. Hammel," And how about you Rakib, how is your work coming along."

Rakib, "It is going well but there's still lot to do. I believe the life of ISS can definitely be extended. The structure itself appears to be in great shape with no signs of fatigue. The skin-to-frame adhesions and connections are all intact. I am starting to believe that whoever determined the original service life of ISS was too conservative with their calculations or the ISS itself, has not experienced the forces and pressures that were originally anticipated. I believe a commercial airline is subject to more severe conditions than the ISS. But before we go much further, I suggest a thorough external inspection of ISS should be performed.

Capt. Hammel, "Rakib it sound like you are talking about multiple spacewalks. That could take you to some places on ISS that are difficult to get to."
Rakib, "Yes difficult and dangerous but with the proper planning, these external inspections can be done safely and without mishap.

Chapter 5

Alert

"Mission Control, Houston to ISS. Come in ISS".

Rakib, "That's unusual. They don't usually call this late in the evening. What time is it in Houston anyway?"

Gloria, "1:18 AM"

"This is ISS, Capt. Hammel"

"Captain, this is Mission Control's Operation Manager Doug Ryerson on a Zoom call with my second-in-command John White who I think you know, and Roger Halverson of NASA's Astronomical Observation Group (AOG). Roger is the evening shift manager. Captain, we would like to discuss the item I spoke to you about last week."

John White, "Good evening, Frank. I hope we didn't alarm you with this late-night call but, as Doug mentioned, something has come up regarding the item which we are now calling a cloud. To begin with, when the AOG discovers anything new, or of interest in our galaxy, we immediately send out a Notice of Observation or Sighting (NOS) to a subscribed, worldwide list of Radio and Optical telescope operators. It classifies the item or sighting in terms of distance, size, threat level and so on. Estimated location coordinates and a brief commentary may also be included."

John, "Roger will fill you in on what's turned up."

Roger Halverson, "Two days after we sent out our NOS, we were contacted by the Cerro Paranal Observatory located in the High (8,645 ft.) Andean desert, at San Pedro De Atacama, Chile. It is operated by the European Southern Observatory (ESO) organization." Due to its location in the lower southern hemisphere, ESO Chile as it is known, has the ability to view parts of the galaxy that are often missed by other observatories positioned further in the northern areas of earth. After reviewing our NOS and the approximate location coordinates of the item or cloud, they decided to take a look.

What they found concerns us. The Chileans did have a clearer and more direct view of the item, and they were able to conclude that it is a gas cloud containing very fine particles of dust or ash. They could not determine if anything larger, say small meteor fragments or other types of solid space debris, are "hidden" inside. A radio telescope observation will answer that question. ESO Chile has an excellent one and they are preparing to take a "look" as we speak.

The Chileans estimate that the speed of this mass to be between 15,000 to 25,000 thousand miles per hour. It is headed in the general direction of Earth and the ISS. They say it is too early to determine an accurate heading or ETA. They did report that it is not very large in size, perhaps 20 to 50 miles in diameter, with a 50-to-100-mile "halo" surrounding it. The glow is what makes them believe that it's a gas cloud. But at this point it is only an educated guess. Mission control and NASA are checking the data supplied by the Chileans and we will let you know of any changes."

Doug Ryerson, "Thank you Roger."

"Frank, based on this new information and out of an abundance of caution, I think we have some precautionary work to do. For starters you should start reviewing ISS' existing evacuation plans and procedures. We will do the same down here. If you need help with any of the information, just let us know. That goes for anything else that may come up. John will be the point man in Houston. We will advise you what space vehicle we will use to get you down here if an evacuation is necessary. We should know this in several hours. A second priority is that you make certain that all project and experiment data has been sent to Houston. I know data back-ups are done every 6 hours, but it doesn't hurt to check. In particular, look for things that may be outside our normal back-up protocol. We will notify our partners of this situation, and they may also have information / data requests for you to act upon.

Again, please remember that we are taking these actions only out of an abundance of caution and with a little luck this may turn out to be a harmless cloud that pass us by a million miles.

Frank, Gloria, Rakib, do you have any questions for us."

Frank, "I am sure we will. Just give us an opportunity to discuss this among ourselves. We will work this situation on a 24-hour basis with time outs for catnaps and short sleeps. Times is of the essence, and we do not want to wake up 10 days from now and find we have an urgent problem on our hands.

Rakib, "I agree with that."

Gloria, "So do I."

Doug Ryerson, "OK we will sign off now. Talk soon. Oh, one more thing we will keep this "NASA Top Secret" and for now we will not mention it to any family members."

Frank to the crew, "All right now let's finish dinner put our collective thinking caps on and come up with a plan. Thank God we have an evacuation plan that's very complete and one which we practiced 16 days ago. Rakib, please review the plan now and let us know if you have any questions, concerns or if you need any further information regarding its implementation.

And remember, this is still just a precautionary operation, so let's take our time, be through and remember there are no dumb questions. If anything concerns you, ask. And don't panic; everything we are about to do has been well practiced and will work."

Rakib, Gloria, "Aye Aye, Captain"

Rakib, "We're happy to have you leading us in all of this Captain."

Chapter 6

The Luncheon

Patty, "There sure were enough diamonds and jewelry on display at the luncheon today. I guess NASA pays their executives quite well".

Asha, "I Also saw a fair amount of designer clothing."

Patty, "I think it's very nice that Ashly Sosa invited us to the luncheon. It is a show of appreciation and acknowledgement for the work are husbands are doing."

Asha, "Yes, I agree. Plus, the food was good. I liked the curry entree, but it tasted more American than Indian. I see you ordered it too. How did you like it?"

Patty, "I liked it. As a matter of fact, I would order it again."

Asha, "Well, in that case, I will take you to an Indian restaurant where you can have a real Curry spiced dinner."

Patty, "You had the groups' attention when you talked about the Bhopal Citizens Health Mission in India. I think we all realize that in the poorer regions of the world, both medical and nutritional aid are sorely needed. It's great that you are involved with the mission's work. Can you tell me a little more about it? Asha, "Bhopal is where I am from. It is my home. It has never been the same since the chemical plant accident. The Bhopal disaster, or Bhopal gas tragedy, was an industrial accident. It happened at a pesticide plant on the night of December 2, 1984. The plant accidentally released approximately 40 tons of toxic methyl isocyanate (MIC), exposing more than 500,000 people to the toxic gas. The final death toll was estimated to be between 15,000 and 20,000 people. Some victims died immediately, others died months and even years later. At the time, it was called the worst industrial accident in history. We lost part of our population due to evacuations. People never came back because of employment migrations to other more prosperous regions of India. A number of businesses also closed and have never reopened. It has never been the same since the accident. There continues to be a high rate of unemployment. The city itself has never returned to pre-accident conditions. In the beginning, the chemical company did help but they don't seem to be doing much anymore. I guess I can't blame them entirely; they can't be expected to support the economy and the people forever. Some people did receive compensation and damage settlements, but they took the money and ran. I can't say I blame them.

I visit once a year for about 6 weeks, to offer firsthand assistance. My family remained in Bhopal. They are in the manufacturing business. They offer financial assistance to the Mission but much more is needed."

Patty, "Have you thought of setting up a charitable organization in the states to generate some funding for the Mission? I'll bet some of those women we met at the luncheon today would be willing to offer financial support."

Asha, "Yes, I have but I think that would require a full-time commitment especially for start-up and I don't have the time right now. But I will continue with my involvement.

Can I drop you somewhere or do you want to go home?"

Patty, "Home will be fine. I have taxi duty today for a soccer game and I'm teaching a CPR class tonight at the Civic Center.

"Today was a kind of an odd day for me. I just can't stop thinking about Frank. I can't put my finger on why. I'm sure he and the rest of the crew are safe and so far this mission has been quite normal. I'm glad we only have four months before they're back on the ground.

After this mission, I don't know what's next. Frank said that part of him wants to continue with the space program, but it does take him away from home and family. After a while that really seems to wear on him. I think he may get a job on earth, it seems funny to say that. It would definitely involve flying an airplane. He probably would stay with the Air Force and volunteer for flight duty somewhere. Flying is his passion. It's one of the many things I love and admire about him."

Asha, "Rakib will definitely stay with NASA. He has lofty ambitions, and he plans to pursue them working with NASA-Houston or continuing with his space exploration work. He says the problem with missions like ISS or perhaps even traveling to the moon is that it takes him away from NASA headquarters which limits his exposure to the higher ups and tends to stifle his advancement opportunities. So, knowing him I believe his future is on the ground, here on earth and not flying around in space.

Here's your stop. I enjoyed going to the luncheon with you, perhaps we can meet more often depending upon your schedule at the hospital."

Patty," Yes that sounds like a good idea although I must tell you that I volunteer for as much overtime as I can handle when Frank is away, it acts as a good distraction. I just have to be careful not to neglect my kids which I'm sure I won't because they are so much fun to be with. I love spending quality time with both of them and they're still at an age that they still listen to me, and I want to take advantage of it while it lasts!

Thanks again for the lift and we'll talk soon about a luncheon or perhaps even a dinner outing!"

Chapter 7

ISS History

After the call disconnected from Mission Control there was a brief moment of silence. The three crew members were all in the process of absorbing what was just discussed. There was no fear or panic. It was more about thinking of what needed to be done in the event of an actual evacuation. It was also a stark reminder of just how vulnerable they are, and the ISS. And just how dependent they both are on the help and support of others. Even Gloria, the 3-mission veteran had some apprehensions about the work ahead. They also wished they had more personnel on board to help with the tasks.

One of the biggest jobs was surveying the ISS itself and making it ready for the unlikely possibility of abandonment. The station had a number of passageways, nodes, airlocks, and chambers all of which are interconnected to a central, submarine-type tubular passageway and it was chock full of equipment. Just traveling through parts of it was sometimes a chore.

The ISS measures 396 feet in length, or just about as long as a football field including the end zones. The station has multiple solar panel arrays covering an area of 24,000 sq. ft. It's width is 168 feet, and it weighs about one million pounds or 500 tons. The inside areas have as much "people space" as a six-bedroom house. The station continues to expand as more laboratory, service and living accommodation modules are added. They are completely manufactured and tested on Earth before sending them aloft. Upon arrival at the ISS, connection to the station and utility hook-up are all that is usually required before a module can become operational. Some modules do need connection assistance using complex robotics systems and humans in spacesuits.

Design plans for the ISS were started in the 1980s. Construction of the station itself was started during the 1990s. The first ISS module was launched into space aboard a Russian Proton rocket on November 20, 1998. Two additional modules were launched, and they remained in place but unmanned until the year 2000. All three of these modules were made in Russia.

The first manned expedition took place on November 2, 2000, and the station has been manned ever since, sometimes with just a two man "caretaker" crew. Since the initial exposition, ISS has been expanded to its current size of 36 modules and ancillary equipment. 42 shuttle trips were required to build the station, 36 by the United States and 6 by Russia. Along with the modules, additional cargo trips were made to carry materials, supplies, and solar panels aloft, over 60 trips to date. The station generates all of its own electricity.

The ISS is a marvel of engineering, planning, and development. It stands as a fitting example of what can be done by man when differences are set aside to achieve a common goal.

The ISS is not part of NASA. It is a separate entity operated by 18 partner nations. This is the ISS leadership organization:

- Program Director
- Station Director
- Operation Integration Manager
- Chief of Staff

NASA does play a central role in the ISS program, contributing significant funding and resources. ISS offices are located at the NASA Headquarters building in Houston Texas. The Russian space agency, Roscosmos, is the second-largest contributor to the ISS. They operate a segment of the space station known as the Russian Orbital Segment. The European Space Agency, ESA, is another major partner, contributing both funding and expertise to the ISS project. Japan Aerospace Exploration Agency, JAXA, is also actively involved in the ISS program, contributing technology, research, and crew support.

International Space Station (ISS)

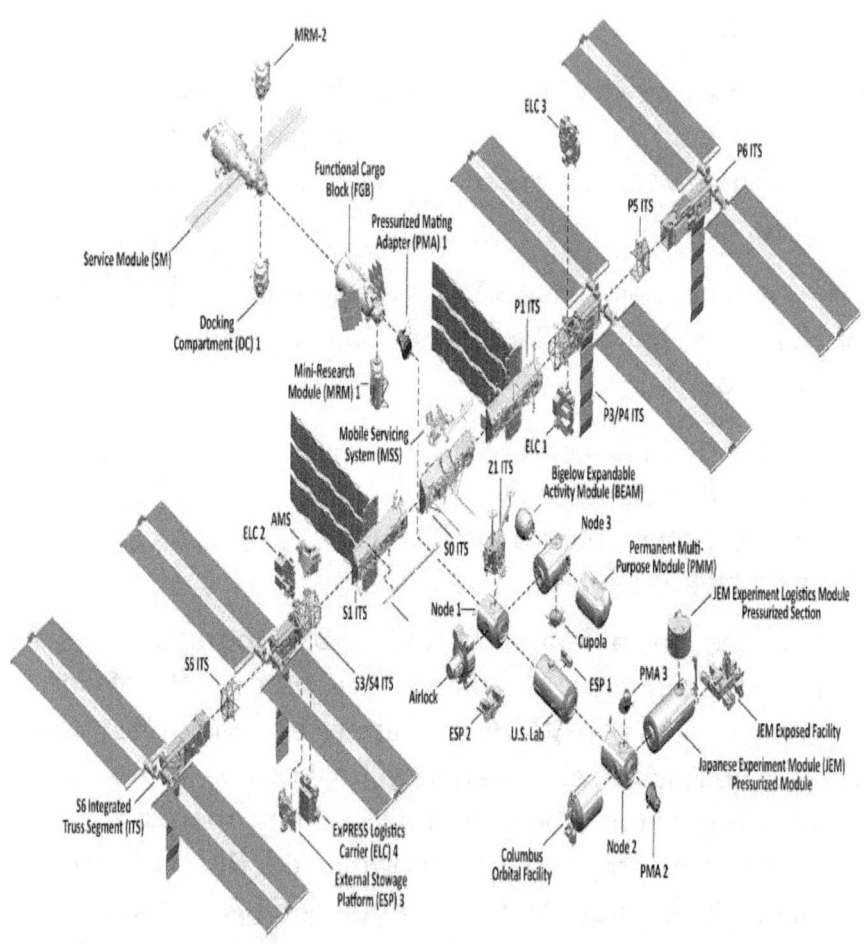

Chapter 8

Evacuation Planning

It is now 12 hours after the initial call from mission control and Captain Hammel has called a crew meeting.

Captain Hammel, "I know we have been talking individually throughout the day, but I wanted to get together to jointly discuss the progress of our evacuation plan. Rakib?"

"I've reviewed the current Evacuation Procedures and have chosen items that apply to our current situation. I have developed a set of instructions that should serve us well if we have to use them. Aside from securing the station, this appears to be a fairly routine departure. You know the station has never gone unmanned since the first crew occupied it in the year 2000."

Captain Hammel, "Yes I know. Do you have anything else?"

Rakib, "Well yes. I did not add this to the plan, trying to keep it simple but, in my travels throughout the station I have also identified several places where, if we had to, we could seek shelter in the event something else happened, say, a possible strike by a foreign object. These places are of stronger construction and offer better protection than the main module bodies. I have made a list. But, as I said I didn't include them in the evacuation procedure because I don't think they'll be needed. I am a little surprised a listing like that didn't already exist. That's about it from me."

Captain Hammel, "And what about you Gloria?"

"I have resent all current and previous data files to Houston. I found some personal effects that have been left behind by previous crew members. I think we should leave them because even if in the event of an evacuation, we or someone else, will be returning so no need to take them with us now. I was going to mention one thing that I thought was a bit odd. As you know we have this little used "text message" function which is connected to our communication system. It is supposed to be used for personal use only. About 4 hours ago I received a text message from Vladimir Krosnick, I think he is the flight director or something for Roscosmos, the Russian space agency. He asked me to send, directly to him, copies of all flight data logs, including arrivals and departures for the last 7 years.

Of course, I did not take any action, but I wanted you to know about it. "Captain Hammel, "That's very interesting although I'm not sure what to make of it. NASA sent a Partner Notice, (PN) out about 10 hours ago. So, the Russians know we are developing a plan of possible evacuation and that probably figured into Roscosmos' request. But why the 'back channel' communication? They knew they could get the information from ISS Houston. And why contact you Gloria? Do you know this guy"?

Gloria, "No, but I've collaborated with their scientists over the years, so they certainly know my name. But they would also know I have nothing to do with flight data or trips to and from the station."

Captain Hammel, "OK. Don't do anything. I'll run this past NASA security and see how they want to play it. And please let me know if you hear anything else."

Gloria, "Aye-Aye Captain."

Captain Hammel, "Does anyone have anything else? If not, I am going to call NASA and give them an update on our progress and see what's new on their end."

"No Captain, That's it"

Captain Hammel, "Mission Control from ISS. Come in Mission Control Houston."

Mission Control, "This is John White, Mission Control Houston. We hear you loud and clear Captain Hammel.

Captain Hammel, "I'm calling for the 8:00 PM update on the evacuation plan. I have sent a detailed report of what we have developed. I take it you have reviewed it. In summary we're good to go. We have a plan and are ready to execute whenever necessary. In addition, we have surveyed the station, sent the necessary data files to Houston and now it is simply a matter of waiting to see what the object out there does.

John White, "Yes, captain, we have received all the data files and have reviewed your plan. Everything looks in good order as far as the evacuation goes.

Captain Hammel, "The only thing missing in our plan is our ride home. How are you making out with that? I was hoping that by now you would have a vehicle name and a launch date."

John White," Actually, we thought we'd be further along with the return home vehicle. As you know, the Russians we're supposed to make the next shuttle trip to deliver their two crew members to ISS. They reported problems with their Soyuz space shuttle and their trip is on hold. They have yet to schedule a future, rocket-ready launch date. U.S. intel believes that the delay is actually due to our involvement with the war in Ukraine which I think you agree is very much a proxy fight between the United States and Russia.

We have talked to the Japanese, and they understand the urgency of the situation, but they just don't have a vehicle even close to ready. Our private contractors in the US seem to be our best option right now and we are working diligently with them to come up with a suitable vehicle. They hope to have something in the next 24 to 48 hours.

We are concerned about the lack of a return shuttle as I'm sure you are. But we have time, and we are optimistic about having a vehicle, or at least a plan to get one, very soon. This is not anywhere near an impossible situation. However, it is a delay, and we are working on it full time. Unfortunately, there's just not a lot of space vehicles or shuttles available that can make a round trip to the ISS."

Captain Hamill, "I don't know what else to say. I know you're working on the problem with all hands-on deck, and we feel confident that you'll come up with a solution.

What about the object itself, the thing that is causing all of our concerns. Is there anything new regarding its position, velocity, heading?"

John White, "Actually Frank there is. The calculations made by our NASA folks indicate that the object may be passing us at a further distance then the Chileans indicated. However, they do have the best line of sight on the object, and we are trying to reconcile the two calculations. We should have some results within the next several hours. But if we're right and the object does pass further from us than was originally reported, my next order will be to tell you to stand down. In the meantime, if your work on the evacuation is complete then I suggest that you get some rest and go back to a normal work routine, and we will keep working on a ride. That's about all I have, Frank. Do you have anything else?"

Captain Hammel, "I have sent an encrypted report to NASA Security. Have you heard from them?

John White, "No I have not."

Captain Hammel, "I suggest you get a hold of them and get the details. They may want us to take some action, and you should be in on it. Also, it may somehow be tied into the Russians being a no-show on their shuttle trip to ISS.

Otherwise, we have nothing further. This transmission was one of mixed messages and I know you folks are doing everything humanly possible to put the evacuation together. In the meantime, we will adopt a wait and see mode.

One final note, we would like you to maintain the news blackout and not contact our families about this. No reason to make them worry unnecessarily.

ISS over and out."

Captain Hammel, "Gloria, Rakib, what do you think of all of this?"

Gloria, "First of all I'm not worried. Having lived aboard ISS for three different times I have certainly come to realize how dependent we are on the folks back on earth. So, I will put my faith in them to get us out of any dilemma that may arise. Besides, we can't do much about it anyway."

Rakib, "I agree with what Gloria said. What surprises me and perhaps aggravates me a little as well is that NASA has no back up plan in the event of a shuttle failure. They have backup plans for everything else but nothing for shuttle back up."

Gloria, "Are you suggesting a spare shuttle parked somewhere on earth just waiting to come to someone's rescue? That would be cost prohibitive!"

Captain Hammel, "We could argue the issue of a spare space shuttle all night and we would not gain anything. I think our best course of action is to be patient and let the folks on the ground manage the shuttle problem. Our job is to work, eat and sleep in as normal a fashion as possible and remember we do have time."

Chapter 9

Leak

Captain Hammel is awaiting the morning situation call from mission control. The last 12 hours aboard the space station have been uneventful with the crew asleep for most of the time but now everyone is awake and awaiting an update from Mission Control.

"ISS from John White, Mission Control Houston. Come in ISS."

"This is ISS, Frank Hammel. Go ahead John."

"Frank, we have some not-so-good news from NASA's Navigation group. They report that the course velocity calculations made by the folks at the Cerro Paranal Observatory are correct. They have also revised the cloud's heading which puts it on a direct course towards ISS, and now that it is closer, the estimated time of arrival in the area of ISS has been moved up. We still have time but not as much as we thought we had. I am sorry to be the bearer of bad news but that is the status of the cloud as of right now."

"John, this is Rakib. Did the NASA guys say why the initial calculations were incorrect."

"They said something about a "slight difference in coordinates." I didn't pursue it because I was focused more on the current calculations which I know are correct. As a double check we had the astronomers at the Mauna Kea Observatory in Hawaii verify them. They came up with the same results. Believe me we've been working on these calculations all night.

On the shuttle front, the news is a little better. We believe that a suitable vehicle has been located. I do not want to say anymore until we are able to check on the details, but it looks very promising."

Captain Hammel, "John, what is the new ETA? Scratch that. We didn't have an old ETA. When is this cloud expected to arrive in our area and do we know its composition?"

John, "The ETA is approximately 12 days from now. We will get more exact times as the cloud gets closer. As far as what it is composed of, it is still looking like gas, ash and space dust or gravel."

"That is all I have for you right now."

"This is Rakib, given your current ETA can you get a shuttle launched, docked and undocked and re-launched back to earth in the 12 day time frame?"

John, "We are working on that as we speak, and our engineers are certain it can be safely done. I'll have more on this after we secure the vehicle."

Captain Hammel, "I'm sure it is getting harder to keep the lid on things, but we would like to continue to keep this news away from our families."

John, "Will do."

The next day the headlines could not have been more blunt. "Meteor Storm To Rain Down On ISS", "International Space Station Facing Grave Danger From Meteors", and "International Space Station Astronauts Face Peril From Meteor Storm" The European wire services were first to break the story, and with no regard for the astronauts' families. Shortly after the object sighting, the ISS Director did have an obligation to advise all of the 18 ISS partners of the event. This added a lot of parties to the information loop but discretion and even secrecy are understood until the ISS director decides to go public with news. But all of our partners are not necessarily our friends.

At NASA and the United States intelligence services, the consensus is that the leak came from Roscosmos. With the proxy war raging in Ukraine, the Russians would jump at the chance to discredit the United States in any way they could and when it comes to propaganda, the Russians are particularly good at it.

But there is a more immediate problem.

"Mission Control to ISS, come in ISS."

Captain, "This is ISS, Go ahead. I hope this is good news."

"Frank, this is John. Listen, the story is out. It started with the European wire service and its worldwide now with all the gory details. We believe the Russians leaked it in an attempt to discredit the United States, to make it look like we do not know what we are doing. But whether or not they are the source, the story is out, and you and your crew should talk to your families about this as soon as possible, hopefully before they hear it on the news. It is 3:00 AM here in Houston so you may have a chance. I have set up the 3 personal links and they are ready so you Rakib and Gloria can talk to your families any time you wish. I am sorry this came out; we tried our best to keep it quiet, but as more and more people got involved it became almost impossible. I will let you go now so you folks can talk to your families.

"John, is there anything new on the arrival time of the cloud or the shuttle?"

"Nothing new on the ETA. The shuttle prospects are looking better but I don't want to say anything just yet."

"OK ISS over and out"

Captain Hammel, "Well Gloria, Rakib you heard both sides of that conversation, I guess we have some phone calls to make. I take it you know how to use the personal link feature. Call mission control and they will patch you into whatever phone number you wish.

"Yes Frank we know how to use the link."

"Ok then I will leave you to it."

"Patricia Hammel? This is mission Control operator Susan. I have a personal call from Captain Frank Hammel aboard the ISS. Go ahead."

"Hi, Patty, this is Frank. Sorry to wake you in the middle of the night but we have a situation with the station, and I wanted to tell you about it before you see it on TV or started getting phone calls."

"Frank, are you in any danger?"

"I don't think so. Let me tell you what's going on. Several days ago, a cloud containing gas, dust, and particles appeared near the outer limits of our deep space surveillance equipment. The cloud was extremely far away. We started to watch it as did several other observatories. A couple of days ago an observatory in Chile determined that the cloud may be heading our way. So, we started to do some 'just in case' type work which includes a review of our evacuation plan. Long story short, the plan is fine, but we don't have a firm commitment for a shuttle to get us out of here, if we need it. In the meantime, the cloud is continuing to move towards us."

Patty, "When is it supposed to get there?"

Frank, "In about 12 days."

Patty, "Can't you just move out of its way?"

Frank," I wish it were that simple. The station has thrusters to keep it in orbit, but they really can't move it any distance nor at any speed."

Patty, "Didn't you once tell me that the station travels about 17,000 miles per hour? I mean, how much speed do you need?"

Frank, "That's its orbit speed . . . It's complicated but it won't work."

Patty, "So what's next; what's going to happen? I'm starting to worry."

Frank, "NASA is optimistic about finding a shuttle. When they do, they will come and pick us up."

Patty, "Like where are they looking? Carvana or someplace like that? I'm sorry, I'm being sarcastic, and I don't mean to be. What you're telling me is making me nervous."

Frank, "NASA is working on this whole problem with all of their available resources. Unfortunately for you and for me we just have to wait and see. I'm going to talk to them as soon as I finish this phone call.

Right now, we have to be strong, you for the kids and me for the crew and the mission."

Patty, "I agree, but it's not going to be easy."

Frank, "The next thing I would like you to do is tell the kids as soon as they get up. Then call the school and tell them about the situation and, this is most important, tell the kids and the school not to believe all of what they hear on television or the internet. They should listen to the NASA press conference; they will have the facts.

Rakib and Gloria had similar conversations with their families.

Rakib's wife said she had just gotten a call from her mother in India about the news after seeing it on BBC-India. Her mother said that she and her father were making plans to fly to Houston to be with her while the story played out.

Gloria talked to her parents. They too had seen the story from a Taipei news feed that they subscribe to at their home in San Diego. Their mood of questioning turned dire, and, at one point, Gloria had to remind her dad that she wasn't dead yet and that prospects for her survival were excellent. He ended the conversation by saying how proud he was of all her accomplishments including her three trips to the space station. And then added a Chinese proverb that said, "At birth we bring nothing; at death we leave with the same." Gloria was not frightened or offended by this because she knew her father was 'old school' Chinese and quoting proverbs was just part of their culture.

The NASA press conference, held at 9:00 AM was brief with just salient details and a timeline of events. Their comments were factual. A few press questions were answered, and NASA offered assurances that more information Would be forthcoming later in the day.

The mood on ISS was subdued. Captain Hammel was trying to be upbeat but in the absence of a shuttle ride back to earth it was difficult to be positive.

Gloria," You know several of my friends told me I was tempting fate by coming here for a third time, but I told them that I don't believe in that kind of stuff. It's like telling an airline pilot not to take more than a certain number of flights. It's just foolish."

Rakib, "I still can't believe that NASA or the ISS group did not build something into their plans that would have some type of shuttle or vehicle at least at the ready to avoid stranding a crew on the ISS. I am not necessarily talking about a spare but at least an existing shuttle that is ready to go.

And another thing, when the Russians advised us of problems with the Soyuz shuttle, NASA or ISS should have pressed them for a detailed explanation and a timeline for their expected readiness date. And NASA or ISS should have found a suitable replacement right then and there. There are a lot of unanswered questions and in the meantime, here we sit, waiting for what. And how about some information on just what the cloud is. Is it just all gas and ash? The station could possibly survive a hit of that material. Or does it contain hard solid objects that will actually damage the station? Mission control should at least give us an answer to that question. Captain, will you please ask that question during your next call?"

Captain Hammel, "That is a good question, and I will ask it.

Chapter 10

Shuttle is Found

ISS from John White, Mission Control Houston. Come in ISS."

"This is ISS, Frank Hammel. Go ahead John."

"Frank We have located a shuttle, and we believe it will be ready in three days."

"Where did you find it John?"

John, "In New Mexico and it's on its way to the Kennedy Space Center right now, being driven there aboard an extra wide truck. We do have some roadway coordination problems, like bridges and underpasses but the transportation guys say they will figure those out."

Frank, "How did this come about?"

John, "Well there is a space vehicle development company that works out of the White Sands New Mexico Proving Grounds that has been developing a more efficient and

54

economical, round trip space vehicle. I believe Space X is in the process of buying them. "The vehicle is fully assembled and has passed all of the NASA pre-flight testing protocols."

Frank, "So it's never flown before?"

John, "No but this company has an excellent development record and a number of former NASA guys working for them. Are you alone?"

Frank, "Yes."

John, "I have to tell you, as of right now, this is the only game in town."

Frank, "Roger that. What's next."

John, "We get the vehicle to Kennedy, set it on a launch pad, run through all of the launch testing and protocols and we will be ready to go.

Frank, "And you're going to do all of this in four days,"

John, "Or less! Oh, there's one more thing. This vehicle will be unmanned. It is designed to save weight. All robotic controlled. Sort of like a state-of-the-art drone. You may recall we have sent unmanned shuttles to the station on a number of occasions; 2 of them were from this company."

Frank, "As I recall there were a couple of unmanned trips that never got off the launch pad."

John, "Yes, but that was in the early days. Since then, significant progress has been made with unmanned and drone technology. Of course, we are still looking for a more conventional, manned shuttle, but in the meantime, we wanted to have something just in case. Me, personally. I hope we don't even need it. We are calling it "Rescue 1" and I will give you updates once it arrives at the Cape."

Frank, "OK, I'll brief the crew, and I am sure they'll want to make some calls home, as will I.

Has NASA released any news?"

John, "They are preparing to do that right now. I'd say you have about 20 minutes to make your calls if you want to beat them to the punch. NASA needs to say something positive. They are getting killed in the press, worldwide. The news reporting goes from accusations of poor management and lack of preparedness at NASA to outright doomsday scenarios. And a lot of the reporting is full of false and misleading statements."

Frank, "OK will talk soon. ISS over and out"

Chapter 11

Cloud Change

The news about finding a shuttle was well received in all three of the astronaut's households.

Patty Hammel and Asha Rakib talked on the phone, first about their relief and then about the fear and foreboding they both felt but tried to hide from their children and their family.

Gloria Fan's family was elated and happy to share the good news with their extended Taiwanese family in San Diego.

At their press conference, NASA did not share much detail about the shuttle find and no one seemed to care. What was on everyone's mind was that a shuttle ride back to Earth had been arranged and the astronauts would be home long before the cloud was even close to the area occupied by ISS. What was almost lost in the excitement was that the ISS itself could still be in harm's way and if lost, it would be a tremendous blow to space exploration.

"ISS from John White, Mission Control Houston. Come in ISS."

"This is ISS, Frank Hammel. Go ahead John."

"Frank, we have an update on the, the cloud. A new trajectory indicates that its path will bring it even closer to ISS, almost dead on and It is also moving, 5,000 miles faster than previously believed. We can still get you off the station in plenty of time, but the speed increase does reduce our safety margin by almost 2 days. But that's still leaves us 9 days to get you out of there".

Frank, "John, these changes are starting to concern me."

John, "Me too Frank. The reason for this change is the object is starting to appear more and more like a gas cloud than a solid object so calculating its speed is not as precise, plus it's still over 6 million miles away.

Frank, "I understand. Do you have a launch time yet?"

John, "No but the shuttle should arrive at the Kennedy Space Center early tomorrow morning and be set up on the launch pad by late tomorrow evening. NASA Techs will immediately start launch protocol checks and pre-flight testing. The entire process should take 2 to 3 days max. Launch will follow ASAP. We are hoping to dock at ISS about 48-60 hours after launch." So, it looks like from right now to docking completion is 5 days".

Sending a shuttle to the ISS is a complex, highly technical operation consisting of six major steps. It usually takes 2-3 days to complete.

Shuttle Launch Sequence

1. Rocket Liftoff

The liftoff phase of a rocket is the point in its launch when it leaves the ground and begins to ascend into space. It takes about 3 minutes to reach space, an altitude of 62 miles per NASA definition.

2. Orbit Activation

The orbit activation phase of a rocket is the process of transitioning from a suborbital trajectory to an orbital trajectory. The orbit activation phase typically lasts approximately two minutes.

3. Phasing Burns

This phase is used to fine-tune the rocket's trajectory and ensure it reaches its destination safely. During phasing burns, the engines are fired in short bursts to make small adjustments to the rocket's course. The time it takes to do this varies depending on a number of conditions.

4. Approach Initiation

This step is the start of a shuttle's initial approach to the ISS. It begins once the shuttle has reached orbit and is about to start its journey to the space station. The rendezvous timeline is based on the space station's orbit, so it's important to make sure that both orbits are accurately calculated. Again, the time it takes to do this varies.

5. Proximity operation

The proximity operations phase of a shuttle going to the ISS is the most dangerous part of the mission. Proximity operations are very risky because there is a danger of collision between the shuttle and the ISS. To avoid this, the shuttle must be carefully maneuvered into position by the pilot or the ground crew if the shuttle is unmanned.

6. Docking and Pressurization

Docking connects the two spacecrafts together. The shuttle connects to the ISS by using a docking port, which is like a giant plug that fits into a socket. Once the two spacecrafts are connected, the pressurization process begins. Pressurization is the process of equalizing the air pressure between the shuttle and ISS. This allows the astronauts to pass between the two vessels.

Frank, "How fast a turnaround do you figure at the space station?"

John, "I figure about three hours after you board and spring launch away. It should take another 3-4 hours to get you back on earth. So, from right now we have about a 4 day safety margin."

It takes about 3.5 hours for astronauts to return to Earth from the ISS. The journey starts with the closing of the shuttle's hatch then it is spring launched away from the station. It is then piloted to a position where it starts to enter Earth's atmosphere. At this point, Earth's gravity starts to 'pull' the shuttle back to earth. As it passes through Earth's atmosphere the shuttle will achieve a speed of about 19,000 miles per hour or 25 times the speed of sound. This is fast enough to break apart the chemical bonds of air molecules, creating an electrically charged plasma around the shuttle. This plasma is extremely hot, and shuttles or spacecrafts need special thermal barriers or heat shields to protect them and their occupants during re-entry. Finally, the shuttle lands on Earth.

Frank, "Timewise, there is not much room for error. But given the task at hand, you folks have done a remarkable job reacting to this problem. Please pass on our thanks on to all who have worked on it."

John, "Will do, but we are not out of the woods yet."

Frank, "Copy that. ISS out"

The rocket and shuttle capsule arrived at Kennedy 2 hours ahead of schedule thanks in part to the various state police agencies along New Mexico – Florida route. Both vessels were quickly erected on lunch pad 39. Launch pre-flight checks were started and an earlier than forecasted launch was expected.

The press has done a 180 degree turn, from major criticisms of NASA and doomsday prediction about the space station and the astronauts to one of praise for all involved.

The families of the astronauts were elated. The two wives each commented on just what an emotional roller coaster this has been for all involved. They are most anxious to see their husbands back on earth and home. Gloria Fan's family shares this feeling.

Work on the shuttle at the Kennedy Space Center is continuing around the clock and is expected to finish on time. The cloud seems to have picked up slightly more speed but should not affect the safety margin by much. Waiting for launch time is becoming almost unbearable. Everyone, family, friends, the worldwide public, and the whole of NASA just want the shuttle to launch as soon as possible.

Chapter 12

The Launch

Three days have passed and launch day has arrived. One of the largest "watch crowds" have assembled around the Kennedy Space Center, Meritt Island, and the surrounding area. It is a Saturday, so the crowd size is even larger than usual.

It has also turned into a media frenzy with news reporters and camera crews from around the globe lining up to get their shots and their stories. A handful of politicians and celebrities are also on hand. The time is 7:13 AM, about an hour to launch time.

The fact that it is an unmanned flight gives the launch a less human feel. There are no pre-launch interviews, no photos of smiling faced astronauts walking to the launch pad transport, no waves or good luck salutations, just a rocket/shuttle combination sitting on a launch pad waiting to be fired up and sent off to the space station.

At ten minutes before launch, utility hoses and cables are disconnected from the rocket and the support gantry is rolled to the rear of the launch pad. A very large display clock which faces the crowds shows the time to launch at 8 minutes, 23 seconds and counting.

It is a beautiful clear and sunny, albeit humid, Florida morning with the temperature at 74 deg. A perfect day to watch a space shuttle launch. Especially this launch because three lives are depending upon its success.

3 – 2 - 1, the rocket ignites. There is an immediate plume of water vapor and orange flames. The sound of the rocket firing arrives at the crowd's edge about a half-second later followed by lift off. The roar from the crowd competes with the sound of the rocket's engine.

In nine seconds, the rocket and shuttle are already 1,400 feet off the ground, but something seems amiss. Veteran rocket launch watchers see it first, a slight wisp of white vapor emanating from the rocket about halfway up its right side. It becomes more pronounced. Three seconds later, with the rocket at 2,400 feet, the vapor stream ignites and the rocket pitches to its left side. A moment later the bottom half of the rocket is totally engulfed in flames. It then loses speed and plunges into the Atlantic Ocean about a mile from shore.

Everyone watching is stunned at what they witnessed. News reporters are at a loss to say what just happened other than the rocket and shuttle that were on a rescue mission to save three astronauts from a possible collision with a meteor cloud, just crashed into the ocean. The silence of the crowds is incredible.

Reaction to the crash was swift. Patty Hammel, wife of ISS commander Captain Frank Hammel, was at home watching the launch with family and friends. A collective gasp went through their den. Her two children ran to her, and she hugged them dearly. Some of the others in the room started crying.

Patty immediately knew what the consequence of the crash was. She and Frank had talked about what would happen if for some reason the shuttle did not make it to the space station. She brought up the subject and at first Frank tried to dismiss it, but Patty insisted they talk about the possibility of a shuttle no-show. Frank told her that without a shuttle rescue, their only hope was that the cloud would miss the space station completely or that it was composed of only gases with no solid, space station puncturing material. The sight of the failed launch horrified her.

Asha Rajbir's mother and father made it to Houston from India. They were at home with her and their 2 grandchildren. Rakib and Asha just talked the night before. They were very upbeat about the rescue mission and the fact that he was coming home earlier than expected. Failure or even delay of the shuttle never entered their conversation. Indeed, when Asha's parents saw the fiery crash of the shuttle, they were thankful that no one was killed. It was only after Asha explained the ramifications of the crash did they realized the gravity of the situation. The children did understand because the rescue mission was the main topic of conversation in both of their schools. Concern and sadness then settled over the house. Asha hugged everyone and then retired to her bedroom where she silently wept.

Gloria's family also watched the launch on TV. For the last 5 days they were intently following the pre-launch stories on TV, and they had spoken to Gloria as recently as yesterday afternoon. They were acutely aware of what the failure of the rescue mission meant and how dire this made the situation. It was the worst case scenario they feared but never discussed. Mr. Fan shut the TV off and silence and sadness prevailed at the Fan household.

Chapter 13

Safe Haven

NASA Director Ernesto Sosa called an emergency Board of Directors meeting to assess the situation and determine their next course of action.

Director Sosa, "I would like to know what just happened out on Launch Pad 39 but it is not our top priority because it will not help our current situation. Our top priority is to get our three astronauts off ISS before the meteor cloud hits it. Here are my questions.

Do we know anything more about the cloud's composition?

Are there are any changes to the heading or speed of the cloud?

What is its latest ETA?

Are there any shuttles in the world that may be available to make a rescue?

The station has thrusters that are used for orbit adjustments; can they be used to move the station out of harm's way?

Who wants to start? I see we have some non-director folks in the room so if you are going to speak, please state your name and your connection to NASA."

"Sir, my name is John White I'm the Manager of the Astronomical Observation Group (AOG). With me is Roger Halverson, he is also with AOG. Roger has been tracking the cloud since it was first observed. He will give us the latest information about the object, Roger."

"Thank you, John. We still believe the object is more cloud-like than solid mass. We feel it is made up of inert and flammable gases. Solids, such as ash and space dust, and some granular materials are also part of its make-up. It may contain some larger, solid particles but so far, we have not detected anything.

This cloud appears different than any others we have seen. For example, our analytical equipment is giving us some unfamiliar profile information, and the gas compositions keep fluctuating. But it is the lack of solid material that puzzles us the most. We have seen and even examined a number of space clouds. They almost always contain some sort of solid material, i.e., meteor fragments or splinters, space rocks and so on. These solids are usually very hard, carbon like material containing irregular shapes and edges. If they are present in this cloud, these solids, along with the cloud are traveling at 20,000 mph, so any contact with the station will likely cause serious damage to the solar panels and to external ancillary equipment. Punctures or rips to the station modules themselves are a real possibility. The fact that we have not detected solids of any size in this cloud is very unusual.

With the possible threat of a station breech we recommend that the three astronauts "suit up" within 4 hours of estimated contact with the cloud.

The cloud's heading has not changed nor has its size, which is now about 80 miles wide with a halo-like aura that spreads out another 100 miles or so. It looks like the aura is being created by flammable gases which is another unusual phenomenon. We calculate that the cloud is still on a direct course to intersect with ISS. Our speed calculation has been updated and, as we said, it is traveling approximately 20,000 mph. The space station orbits at 17,500 mph so even if the cloud were to contact the station in the same directional orbit, the contact speed would be 2,500 mph. This is the lowest speed scenario and at that rate, the station would still be susceptible to significant damage.

With the revised speed calculation, we figure the initial outlying fragments and gas will reach the space station in approximately 87 hours or just under four days.

I'm sorry that the news is not good, but these are our calculations. We have had them triple checked with 2 observatories and a mathematical think tank at MIT. The results are all the same. That's all I have to report."

Director Sosa, "Thank you, Roger you've answered three of my five questions. Who is next? John, do you have anything else for us."

"Yes, first, the Orbit Adjustment Thrusters (OATs) are small low powered jets that are used to "tweak "the space station back into orbit. Even at 250 miles out in space, the forces of Earth's gravity still have a slight effect or pull on ISS. After a period of several months, the cumulative effects of these pulls start to alter the station's designed orbit. The job of the OATs is to move the station back into this orbit. However, the thrusters have nowhere near the power to move the space station any significant distance or at any appreciable speed.

Second, we've literally scouted the earth for a suitable rescue vehicle with no success. Usually, two or three shuttles of various types are ready or nearly ready to fly. We found four but all are inoperable for one reason or another. This is an extremely rare situation, but there is no real readiness coordination between rocket/shuttle builders and operators.

It is the Russian's turn to have a shuttle ready. But they claim to have problems with their Soyuz rockets. Three weeks ago, they even missed sending two of their Cosmonauts back to the ISS. We have no idea of the status of Russia's rockets, and we have not heard anything from them in terms of help or assistance. We really believe they're playing a very dangerous political game, but we have no proof, just a hunch. Just thinking out loud we thought perhaps a call from our president to his Russian counterpart might get some better information. But the phone call might also be used by the Russians for another attempt at negative publicity. Another possibility is the Russian space equipment may really not be working. Just look at the sorry state of their military equipment. But we are not politicians or diplomats so we don't really know if working through political channels will get us anywhere.

In summary we have not been able to locate a replacement shuttle, and we are out of options."

Director Sosa, "So, the bottom line is the cloud is still headed towards the ISS, and we have no way to evacuate our three astronauts. And as a dire consequence, and barring some kind of miracle, our three astronauts are in imminent danger of being killed by a mysterious space cloud we know little about.

I am sorry to be so blunt but that is the situation.

And, as a further consequence, the ISS may be lost to the global space exploration and scientific communities. This whole situation is just horrible.

There are three things that NASA must do.

Continue our efforts to find a way to get Frank Hammel, Rakib Rajbir and Gloria Fan home.

Give the three astronauts the best support we can by working with them to come up with the best 'shelter in place' area on ISS.

Contact the three astronauts and their families and advise them that we are working as hard as humanly possible to come up with a solution to this problem and also to remind them they and their families have the full support of the NASA organization".

Director Sosa continues, "Doug Ryerson, have you been the station contact on this?"

"Actually, no sir, John White has been the contact since the start of the object sighting."

"OK John, you make the call to the station. Please let me know how it went. When the crew has finished making their calls home, please let me know because I would like to make a follow up call to each of the astronauts and their families.

Has anyone heard from the space station? By now they must know the shuttle won't be arriving."

John, "Not yet sir, I am going make a call to the station right now.

Director Sosa, "Very well."

Worldwide news reaction to the launch failure was almost instantaneous. Headlines again ranged from criticism to outright condemnation of NASA. Stories reported accusation and finger pointing, including blaming the space agency for taking short cuts and having an outright disregard for safety compliance in order to get the shuttle airborne.

There were some articles expressing concern and sympathy for the astronauts and their families and hope that somehow, they would be rescued. But unfortunately, others ran morbid countdowns and timelines remaining before impact and what would happen to the astronauts and the space station after the crash. Most of these stories contained errors, false statements, and misleading commentaries all meant to sensationalize the reporting. But many people believed them. One such story claimed that after the crash, fiery pieces of the space station would be visible to the naked eye as they rained down to Earth. Another asked for money and prayers that God or extraterrestrials might intervene and save the astronauts.

The first thing John White did when he got to the Mission Control Room was to double check that all future calls to the ISS were encrypted. Future discussions with the station were much too sensitive to be spied upon by the press or other publicity seekers.

"Mission Control from ISS come in ISS this is John White."

"Go ahead Mission Control this is Captain Frank Hamill."

"Frank, this is John."

"John, where's our ride home? What's the delay? We're about to call Uber!"

"Frank I'm afraid I have some bad news about that. The shuttle exploded about 24 seconds after liftoff. It looked like some kind of fuel tank leak caused the explosion."

"I get the feeling there's more."

"There is. We don't have another shuttle to send up for you. We've looked everywhere, worldwide, and cannot locate an operating shuttle."

"What does this mean where does this leave us."

"Needless to say, we will continue our search, but as of right now it looks like you'll have to remain aboard the space station while the cloud passes. NASA engineers are already looking to identify a 'safe haven' aboard the station for you to seek the most advantageous shelter. We will send you our list ASAP."

"John, you know one of our astronauts on board, Rakib, is doing a study about extending the useful service life of ISS. As part of his work, he has done an extensive survey of the structures and modules of the space station. He has also identified a number of places of stronger than usual construction that could be considered 'safe havens'. NASA engineers should call him after they have developed their list.

Can you give us an update on the cloud?"

"Yes, it's heading, and speed haven't changed. It should arrive at the space station in about 86 hours. Our concern is what's inside the cloud. The experts say it probably contains ash and dust along with some solid material. It's the solid material that might do harm to the station."

"What level of harm are you talking about?"

"There is a very real possibility that the station will experience punctures and rips or tears in the modules skin. Solar panels and other external equipment could be severely damaged."

"Assuming we and the station survive contact, what happens next? We still don't have a shuttle, or ride home."

"The simple answer is we will work until we get one and then we will come and get you."

"John, what are the odds we survive the collision, or crash, or interception, or whatever it is."

"Frank there's no good way to say this; the odds of you and the station escaping heavy damage are not very good.

Going back to the 'safe haven' discussion NASA, feels that is your best chance for escaping harm."

"You mean the best chance for surviving, don't you?"

"Yes, I momentarily forgot who I was talking to.

"So, the overview is, there's no shuttle pickup before intersecting with the cloud. Our best action is to shelter in place in the strongest part of the space station we can find and hope there's enough of us and the station left to facilitate a pickup whenever a suitable shuttle is found. If I were a gambler, I would not take this bet."

"Frank, unfortunately, that is a very good summation. Do you want me to talk to the other members of your crew?"

"No, they have been listening to this conversation. We have some phone calls to make and Rakib has to get with the NASA engineer double quick to settle on our 'safe haven' location. Gloria and I will figure out food supplies, communications equipment, and oxygen and water supplies."

"And Frank you will probably be getting a call from NASA director Sosa to talk about the situation. He has taken the lead on this."

Once again, the crew make phone calls to their family members regarding their perilous situation. The conversations are serious and foreboding with much concern for the loved ones on both sides of this calamity. The calls all end with expressions of love, hope, and consolation.

Director Sosa first called ISS and spoke to the crew. He apologized for NASA's failure for not having a standby shuttle somewhere in the worldwide space exploration community.

He reiterated NASA's ongoing attempts to get the crew home safely either before or after the cloud intersects with the station. He went on to say how hard everyone at NASA, and beyond, are working to bring about a positive outcome and how he secretly wished the cloud would somehow veer off and miss the space station completely. He closed by saying how grateful and thankful he and the NASA family are for the great work the crew has accomplished. His final message was that regardless of the outcome NASA would stand by and take care of their families.

Director Sosa then called the three families of the crew members. He spoke of NASA's continued efforts to bring about a positive end to the cloud dilemma. He told the families how grateful the NASA family, the worldwide scientific community and indeed, the country were of the astronauts and their work in the field of space exploration. He ended, in very somber tones, saying that NASA would be there for them regardless of their needs.

The Media has been relentless in their coverage of the 'ISS Stranding', as they have taken to calling it and the peril facing the astronauts. Any outcome one could think of has been reported, no matter how farfetched or outlandish the story might be. The tone of some reporting has softened and there were biographies written about all three crew members. Gloria Fan was described as an immigrant from Taipei, Taiwan who came to this country on scholarships from several prestigious West Coast universities. Some articles went on to say how, once settled, Gloria brought her mother and father to the U.S. to allow them to retire in the comfort of Southern California. Rakib was also described as an immigrant who came to America after an employment offer from NASA's Space Flight and Exploration Division. He is described as a brilliant engineer who is expected to go places with the space agency. It also mentioned how he brought his wife over from India and started a family in Southern California. Captain Frank Hammel is described as an All-American type who graduated from the Air Force Academy with honors and became a fighter pilot and then an astronaut and who currently is in command of the ISS. Some articles speak about his wife Patty and her work as a nursing supervisor at a local Houston hospital. Other articles mention the astronaut's children and the stress they're all under being subjected to the hype and notoriety that follows a story like this.

It seems the whole world is fixated on this event. Many people die each day in war or accidents or just naturally, but this particular story has really grabbed the attention of the world, perhaps because of the peril that can be foreseen amid the backdrop of the inherent risks and danger of space exploration.

"Mission Control to ISS come in ISS this is John White."

"Go ahead Mission Control this is Captain Hamill,"

"Frank, I wanted to give you an update on the cloud. Its heading and speed have not changed nor has its estimated size. Composition analysis is still hindered by the ash and space dust particles and again we are seeing some unusual profiles from our radio telescopes that we have not seen before with other clouds. The cloud is now 60 hours or about 2 1/2 days from intercept with ISS. How are you doing with the 'safe haven'?"

Frank, "NASA engineers and Rakib agree that the best place to shelter is in the Functional Cargo Block (FGB). It has everything we need, and it actually served as the command center for first control module set up."

The FGB is an ISS module that was originally part of the Soviet TKS spacecraft. It was the first component of the ISS to be launched and functioned as the control room for early ISS development. The control room part of the module is still operational. Currently, the FGB provides functional support in the form of electrical power distribution, propulsion, guidance, and docking. Support for cargo operations is supplied in the form of a pressurized habitable cargo storage section.

John, "How long before you get it prepped and ready?"

Frank' "It should be loaded and ready by tomorrow afternoon. Right now, we are gathering what we think we will need, including three spacewalk suits, and moving it all of it to an area near the FGB. This is quite a chore. Then, in priority order, we will load whatever we can into the module.

The folks at Mission Control have made some good suggestions regarding 'take along' items."

"Frank, is there anything else we can do for you?"

"Nothing I can think of. Tomorrow, we'll wrap up the gathering phase of the plan and start loading the FGB. We are going to make some phone calls and call it a night."

John, "OK, we're here if you need us."

Captain Hammel, "10-4, ISS over an out."

Chapter 14

Raindrops

It is 4:30 AM the next morning aboard the space station. Captain Hammel is awakened by the sound of what he initially thinks are gentle rain drops. But after a few seconds he realizes it does not rain in space, at least not like the rain he is used to on Earth. He rises quickly and notice Gloria and Rakib have also awakened.

Rakib, "What's that?"

Gloria, "Can it be stray meteor shower or some outlying Cloud material that has gone undetected?'

Captain Hammel, "I don't know. I'm going to take a look through the Zvezda module windows. Rakib, put a call into Mission Control and let them know about possible debris field contact."

On his way to the module, Captain Hammel notices that the 'rain sound' is getting louder and more intense.

"Gloria, activate shutter closures on all windows."

"Aye-Aye Captain!"

Upon arrival at Zvezda, Captain Hammel cautiously operates one of the window shutters. The sound of 'rain' is beginning to lessen. As the shutter opens, he sees a field of transparent granules, each about the size of a half grain of rice. He also notices that the space station is moving away from the field. He attributes this to the station's orbital movement. The rain sound is now gone.

"Gloria, Rakib, can you come to Zvezda. I would like you to look at something."

By the time they get to the module and peer out the window, the station has moved a good distance away from the granular field, but it is still visible.

"What do you think? Have you ever heard of or seen anything like this?"

Rakib, "Considering its transparency and sparkly appearance, it could be some form of ceramic silicon nitride which is in the Quartz family."

Gloria, "I would go with Corundum, a crystalline form of aluminum oxide typically containing traces of iron, titanium, vanadium, and chromium. It is a naturally transparent material but can have different colors depending on the presence of metal impurities. Corundum has two primary gem varieties: ruby and sapphire. It is a rock-forming mineral with a hardness rated of 9.0 on the Mohs scale with 1 being the softest and 10, being the hardest. It can scratch almost all other minerals. The only thing harder is Diamond, rated a 10."

Captain Hammel, "Wow thanks for the mineral lesson. If we're facing a cloud full of this stuff we could be in a heap of trouble. I wonder why it went undetected?"

Rakib, "Maybe its stealthiness is because of its transparency."

"I have NASA Calling."

"Thank you, Gloria."

Mission Control said that they too had no advanced warning of the granular field. They agree that the material could be Corundum judging from the hard sound it made as it hit the station and its difficulty to detect, although there are a lot of other strange and unfamiliar materials out in space as well.

They also agreed with Captain Hammel that the orbital movement of the station is the reason for the contact coming and going. In other words, the station moved in and out of the cloud field, but it is still present, meaning the station will orbit back into its path on its next orbit cycle, which is in 72 minutes, (normal time for the ISS to circle the Earth is 90 minutes less 18 minutes since last contact).

This is very concerning to all. Mission Control orders the crew to shelter in the 'safe haven' module, FGB. They are already there; however, they decide to go back out to the adjacent corridor and retrieve some of the supplies and material that they gathered and which they consider essential for survival.

They are now back in the FGB. It is 15 minutes before their next orbit cycling into the cloud's path.

NASA has still not detected anything on their monitoring devices, nor has the space station.

Rakib, "Captain we may be doing this cycling thing for a while because we have no idea how large this undetected cloud is. I hope the station can stand up to multiple contacts with it."

Captain Hammel, "I agree Rakib, and a more frightening thought is, if we are getting this kind of disturbance from something we didn't see, what will happen when the stuff we can see starts hitting us."

Gloria, "Captain, we should make a short list of additional things to gather after this next cycle. We will have almost an hour to do the task."

"That's a good idea, Gloria."

Just about on schedule, actually 87 minutes since the first encounter, the 'rain sound' starts. Almost immediately the sound gets louder and more intense. It's like sitting in a house as a hurricane passes over, but here the consequences are worse. The sound of a metal object careening off the station's hull is heard, and lights flicker on and off several times. More sounds of objects hitting the station are heard and several station alarms are sounding from outside the FGB. This is indeed a scary moment.

About four minutes later the sounds start to lessen and after five minutes there is silence, except for a tapping sound which is believed to be an external piece of equipment, most likely a loose solar panel part, banging onto the station.

Captain Hammel, "I don't believe we have any hull breeches because alarms would be sounding, but we are going to do a brief damage assessment. I don't see any suits."

Gloria, "All three suits are outside the FGB in the corridor. It's going to be difficult to move around inside the space station with the suits on. We were only bringing them in case we had to work outside."

Captain Hammel, "Yes, good point. We will have to take our chances and do the assessment without wearing them. But since there is a risk perhaps, we'll wait for another cycle or two."

Rakib, "Using the time it took to pass through the cloud, 5 minutes, and the orbit speed we are traveling, 17,500 MPH, I figure the cloud path we passed through was an area of approximately 1,450 miles. What we don't know is whether we passed through it lengthwise, widthwise, perpendicular, or what have you."

Right on time, The 'rain' starts again. This time it is much more intense and from the sound of it, more damage is being done to the equipment attached to the outside of the station, especially the solar panels.

Captain Hammel, "Mission Control, this ISS, we are declaring a "Mayday". The station is under siege from cloud debris, and the situation is becoming critical. The crew is holed up in the FGB and we feel a space station breech is imminent."

"ISS this is Mission Control, John White. We copy. Frank, we of course believe you about the debris field, but we are not picking up anything on our radar, or optic or radio telescope systems. Other than telling you to shelter in the FGB, I don't believe there is anything else you can do right now. I really wish there were. We have been working night and day to come up with a solution, but we have nothing. This cloud thing has taken us by surprise, we have never seen anything like it, and quite honestly, we don't even know what we are up against."

Captain Hammel, "John, I understand. Declaring a "Mayday" was to go on record describing the level of our situation. And believe me, we do not blame you or NASA or anyone else for our predicament. This is part of the risk and peril of space exploration, and we all accept and understand that. It is the feeling of helplessness, of not being able to do anything for ourselves, that really bothers us the most."

Chapter 15

The Home Front, Houston

Patty Hamell has sent her two children off to school. Between the media and school, the children have a fairly good idea of the peril their dad is facing. Patty is trying to maintain as much normalcy as possible. She has had some really good conversations with them and has tried to allay their concerns as much as she can. She thinks to herself how lucky she and Frank are to have two great kids and how well they all get along. They are a happy group when they are together.

Patty has decided to visit Asha Rajbir and Wu and Chi-Ling Fan, Gloria's dad, and mom. She feels visiting the other two families may help her, and them, cope with the calamity they are all facing.

Asha is genuinely happy to see Patty. She introduces her to her parents Amyra and Sandeep Singh. They traveled from Bhopal as soon as they heard news of the cloud threat. They wanted to be with their daughter. Sandeep served cups of Masala Chai Tea a traditional Indian beverage served with milk, honey, and spices. They talk about the misfortune created by the 'space cloud' and Asha mentioned the peril Rakib, her husband, and the other astronauts are facing. They console each other with comments of hope; they talk about how proud both families are of Frank and Rakib's accomplishments and they mention how courageous and valiant both men are. The visit ends with hugs and kisses and optimism for a successful outcome.

Wu and Chi-Ling Fan have traveled from their home in San Diego to Houston. They are staying at Gloria's condo and have relatives in the area. Patty is graciously received by the Fans. Again, tea is served, and comments are made about a positive outcome to the 'space cloud' dilemma. Wu fan produces several photo albums he has carried with him. They contain photos of Gloria, certificates of achievements, awards, and diplomas that she has received over her 29 years of life. Among the most moving pieces of memorabilia are photos of Gloria when she was a little girl. Her mother dressed her in the most tasteful outfits to highlight her Asian beauty even as she was growing up. Chi-Lin said she was a seamstress in Taipei, and she made all of her daughter's clothes. They were very proud of Gloria and all she has accomplished and, they added, at such a young age. But above all they wish for a safe and happy end to the 'space cloud' predicament.

Her visiting over, Patty starts for home. These visits have helped her, and she believes they helped the other families as well. But of course, nothing can make the problem go away. As she harbors that thought, she looks skyward and thinks of Frank and the difficulties he and his crew will be facing. Little does she know; the difficulties have already started.

Chapter 16

Severed

On board ISS, the onslaught continues. Initially the cycles were every ninety minutes, but something has changed. The cycle times are now irregular; the intensity has gotten greater, and longer.

The module they are sheltered in is Russian built. it was the first one sent aloft to serve as part of the ISS. It functioned as the original control room and is now used as a backup command center with a full set of controls and monitoring equipment including gauges, dials, sensor read-outs and communication equipment.

The information provided by this equipment is the only way the astronauts have of knowing the position, heading, and speed of the space station. NASA's tracking system also helps with this task. What they are learning is not good. For one thing, cloud winds have changed the station's elliptical orbit from 260 miles above Earth to a height of 300 miles, and they continue to gain altitude. The station's speed has also decreased from 17,500 mph to 12,000 mph probably due to cloud head winds. The station crew and NASA cannot control any of these changes or the movement of the ISS. They are at the mercy of the cloud.

The next cycle is the most intense and severe yet. It starts 10 minutes later than the previous cycles. The astronauts attribute this to the repositioning of the space stations orbit. The debris that start hitting the station are now more like shards or chevron shaped pieces of material. They also sound larger, and they appear to be doing more damage. The station itself is shuddering and shaking. Sudden up and down movements also start for the first time. Several alarms are beginning to sound, and the module's control panel is flashing red lights.

"Station Breech, Station Breech" is announced over the station's warning system. The control panel shows that the breech has occurred in the Japanese Experimental Module (JME).

"Captain, is there anything we should be doing?"

"I'm afraid not Gloria. It would be far too dangerous to go and investigate. We will just have to sit tight and hope we somehow travel out of the cloud's path. We are moving, the control panel now shows that we are 375 miles above earth and the station continues to gain altitude."

Rakib, "My concern is the space station itself and whether or not it will hold up. As you know the station was constructed of many modules and is literally bolted together. It was not designed to withstand the conditions that the cloud is throwing at it."

"Station Breech, Station Breech."

Capt. Hammel, "Another breech! Where is it this time?"

Gloria, "The U.S. Laboratory. The alarm panel is also showing that most of the solar panels are inoperable."

"Station Breech, Station Breech."

Gloria, "This time it's the Harmony Module, Node 2."

The severity of the cycle intensifies. Then two very stronger shutters occur about 3 seconds apart. The FGB module pitches and rolls. More banging is heard followed by several strong shutters and vibrations. Then absolute quiet. The pitching and rolling continues. Most of the control room screens go blank and the lights in the module go dark for about 10 seconds. Emergency lighting is then automatically activated. Only one of the six data screens is displaying information. The other five are dark. The active screen shows a station altitude 4,859 miles; Speed 16,216 mph; heading, 180 Degrees.

Captain Hammel, "Is everyone OK?

Rakib, "Yes"

Gloria, "Yes"

Captain Hammel, "That was some disturbance. I believe our speed increase may be an indication that we have separated from ISS. Also, the five displays that are not reporting information are operating, they are just not receiving any data."

Rakib, "Also our heading changed rapidly, and I doubt the entire station could swing around that fast."

Captain Hammel, "The bad news is, if that heading is correct we are no longer in any kind of orbit around earth but rather traveling in a straight line directly away from earth. Gloria, "And at a speed of over 16,000 mph."

Rakib, "Yes, we can be on the Moon in no time! Sorry, that was a bad joke."

Captain Hammel, "I am going to see if I can call, NASA. I don't know what kind of shape our communication equipment is in."

"ISS to Mission Control. . . . . .ISS to Mission Control. This is Captain Hammel"

Silence. Three more attempts to make contact are also met with silence.

On a lark, Gloria, tries the private communication link. After five rings she hears. "This is NASA Houston. How may I direct your call?"

"Mission Control Please."

"Mission Control, Mike Zubac speaking."

"Don't hang up! This is Gloria Fan of ISS our main communication system is down, and I am calling you on our private communications link."

"Are you kidding me?"

"Absolutely not! May I speak to John White?"

"John is not here."

"How about Doug Ryerson?"

"Yes. He is here"

"Please let me speak to him and don't put me on hold!"

"Doug Ryerson here"

"This is Gloria Fan of ISS our main communication system is down, and I am calling you on our private communications link. Don't ask me how this is working but it is. Stand-by for Captain Hammel."

"Doug? This is Frank Hammel"

"Frank, where are you? We thought the worst after we saw what happened to ISS."

Captain Hammel, "What happened? We don't know."

Doug Ryerson, "It was busted up pretty bad after the last cloud cycle got through with it. Unfortunately, there is nothing left. Parts are scattered all over the galaxy. Some will fall to earth while others will become part of the space junk inventory that orbits around our planet, and some will just drift off into space.

We saw that the FGB was severed from the station and set adrift by the initial cloud contact. That may have saved your life! Where are you now?"

Captain Hammel was able to report heading, and speed, just before communication with Mission Control was lost.

Frank talks to Gloria and Rakib.

"Our situation is not good. The ISS is gone so there is no suitable place to land a rescue craft even if one could be found. To make matters really worse we, as Gloria said, are hurtling away from Earth at 16,000 mph. And we have no means of communicating with anything or anybody back on Earth. I did manage to report our speed, and heading, to Mission Control just before we lost communication, so they probably have some idea of where we are heading. Food and water are more than adequate, but our oxygen supply is limited, and we do not have any oxygen generators in the FGB. Finally, we have no way to heat the module and the temperature outside is a balmy minus 455 deg. below zero. It is getting cold in here already."

Gloria, "Wow, that's quite an assessment! What will get us first, oxygen deprivation or the unbelievably cold temperature?"

Rakib, "Based on speed and heading, I estimate we are already 96,000 miles from earth. I'll say it. This looks like the end for us."

Back in Houston, NASA has come to the same gloomy conclusion. Director Sosa deals with the heart wrenching fact that he and his small army of incredibly talented workers can do nothing more to save the lives of the three crew members. He knows their time is limited and even if they have an ample supply of oxygen, the extreme cold temperature will quickly end their lives.

Director Sosa must now decide how long he must wait before making the calls to the three families.

After double checking the reports as to the time the FGB was disconnected from the ISS and its reported speed, NASA has a general idea where the three astronauts are, and it is very far from Earth. He waits a short time and makes the calls. They are very difficult and heartfelt. He hopes he never has to do anything like that again.

Each family is dealing with their loss in their own way. Fortunately, they have an abundance of relatives, friends and of course the NASA family to offer their help and support. Condolences pour in from around the world and from local and national political figures. But as wonderful and comforting as this all is nothing can really make the hurt go away. That will simply take time, for some longer than for others.

The media too has been kind. Photos, stories, bios, and listings of accomplishments have dominated the reporting. Explanations as to what happened have basically followed the NASA press releases. Finger pointing, blame, accusations, and distortions will surely follow after the last memorial service is held.

Chapter 17

Rescue

An alien spacecraft known to its occupants as Long Range Galaxy Explorer Vehicle 167 (LRGEV167) is currently passing through the Earth's quadrant of the Milky Way Galaxy. This craft is returning to its home planet after a two year expedition of the outer reaches of the Milky Way and also to take a closer look at the Milky Way's nearest neighboring galaxy, Andromeda. LEGEV167's planet or home base is called Grace; it's inhabitants are known as Gracians.

They have been exploring their part of the Milky Way and beyond for thousands of years. Like Earthlings, their early space explorations started with short forays into space using rudimentary equipment and technology. As their intelligence and technologies advanced, their reach into space expanded.

The Gracians' approach to space exploration has been twofold: first, they simply wanted to learn about their surroundings. As their explorations continued, they found that their universe was forever expanding and that it is shared with others. The more they learned the deeper they went into this vast galactic realm they called 'Beyond.' Second, they decided to limit their explorations to only those discoveries that would benefit and enhance their existence and their life on planet Grace. The selectiveness of this criteria led to rejecting a number of places in the Milky Way which they had either visited or closely observed from space.

Earth was one of these rejected places. It had little appeal to the Gracians. They had visited the planet 4 times and each time they witnessed wars, enslavement, and a widespread practice of intolerance towards each other. On each subsequent visit they saw these dreadful conditioning worsening.

To the Gracians, planet Earth seems to harbor a preoccupation with unrest and conflicts that seemed to center around religion or territorial possession. The Gracians felt that the Earthlings could accomplish so much more if they simply worked together.

For example, during their 1943 visit the Gracians did notice significant technological advances from previous visits, but most of them were used to make more advanced weaponry. If they could only commit their resources and scientific research to peaceful development, what a better place Earth would be.

Although the Gracians did not think that Earth had much to offer them, they did not completely 'write-off' the planet.

They decided to put Plant Earth on their watch list and if future explorations passed by Earth, they would monitor communication activities on the warring planet to see if conditions had changed or at least had improved. It was this monitoring practice that alerted the Gracians to the dilemma facing the drifting ISS crew.

The crew of LRGEV167 had picked up and interpreted the stressful communication between the ill-fated ISS and their earth-based counterparts. They learned of the destruction of the ISS and that one of its modules, containing three astronauts, had been set adrift into space. They realized that if nothing was done to help the astronauts they would soon die from the extreme cold of space. The Gracians decide to see what they can do to help their fellow astronauts.

The ISS is now about 310,000 miles above Earth. The Gracian's vehicle is about 275,000 miles beyond that. Getting to a rendezvous point with the ISS will not be difficult for the Gracians but what they can do to help remains to be seen.

Upon arrival at what's left of the station, the Gracians find the module marred and damaged from its encounter with the cosmic cloud. It is drifting off into space and appears to have been literally ripped away from the main ISS structure. This forced detachment probably saved the three astronauts from being destroyed along with the station itself. The Gracians quickly fashioned a makeshift pressure connection to the module and entered it. They find the three astronauts unconscious. A quick examination reveals they are suffering from hypothermia, asphyxia, and were near death. In fact, if NASA doctors examined them, they would probably be pronounced dead. However, the Gracians have advanced medical equipment that can detect the most minute signs of life right down to the cellular level. Remarkably, they do find life signs and realize they are dealing with a very critical situation.

The Gracians quickly call their main exploration vehicle, LEGEV167 the equivalent of a 'mother ship', which is hovering near-by. They have a rescue craft dispatched for assistance with the drifting ISS module. The astronauts are transferred to the rescue craft where Micro-Oxygen Infusion is immediately started. Coincidently, this form of oxygen therapy is remarkably similar to the Micro-Oxygen Plant Infusion (MOPI) experiments Gloria Fan had been carrying out on the space station.

A short time later the three astronauts find themselves in the 'sick bay' of the LRGEV167. All three are still unconscious and barely alive. This medical facility is unlike any seen on Earth. Pathology and X-Ray equipment have been replaced with analytical and scanning devices using digital electronics and laser technology. Most operations, if even necessary, are performed using non-invasive, arthroscopic, laser assisted procedures. This very advanced equipment along with the skill sets of the attending medical staff will mean the difference between life and death for the three astronauts.

Chapter 18

The World of the Gracians

Planet Grace is home to 1.7 billion Gracians. By comparison, about 8 billion people inhabit planet Earth. Grace is located near the Perseus Arm of the Milky Way Galaxy. It is approximately 65,000 light years from Earth. However, Earth's astronomers never observed Grace due to distance and the presence of space dust and debris.

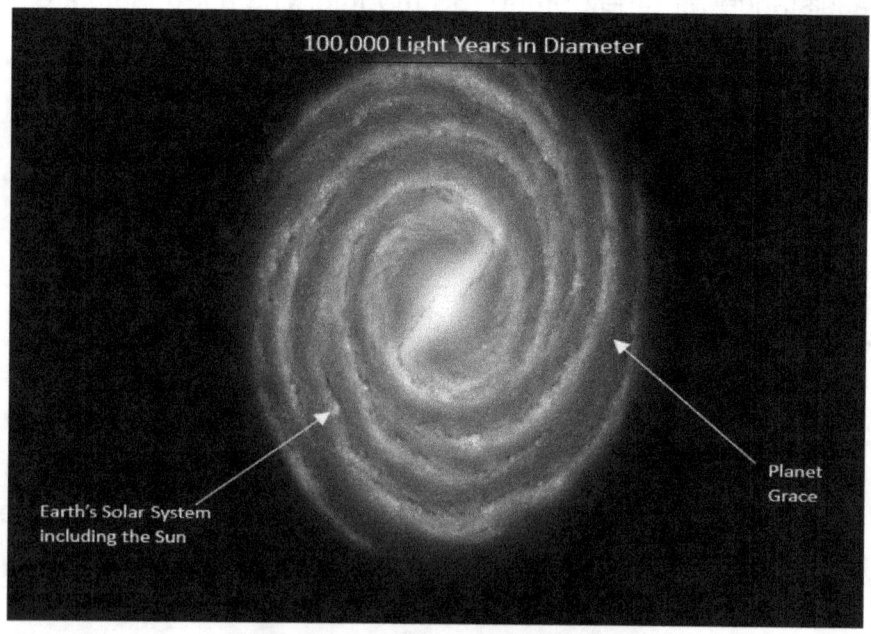

Milky Way Galaxy

The Planet is approximately 7,100 miles in diameter, or about 90% of the size of Earth. It does not tilt on its axis, and it rotates around twin suns. One full rotation takes about 330 earth days to complete. The twin suns provide light and energy which is distributed evenly over the planets' north and south hemispheres during each daytime cycle. The planet spins, like earth and takes about 21.6 Earth hours to complete one cycle which is split equally between night and day or light and dark as the Gracians say. Since there is no tilting axis, Planet Grace enjoys one single season with an average daytime temperature of 77 degrees F. Nighttime temperatures' average 68 degrees F. The climate is subtropical with an average rainfall between 50 – 60 inches. Intermittent breezy periods are experienced but strong winds and rainstorms are a rarity. Water covers about 65% of the planet's surface. There is little ice at either pole and there is no tide differential due to the absence of a moon. Air quality is excellent, and its composition is identical to Earth's.

The Gracians have existed about 5,800 years longer than the Earthlings. This has resulted in a population with far higher intellectual quotients. This higher cerebral capacity combined with a longer existence helped the Gracians create a much more advanced civilization.

All the inhabitants of Grace are of one race. Their features are Anglo Saxon, but the skin tone is more Asian. They are human-like and resemble Earthlings in size and appearance. They are attractive, fit and like most of the population of planet Grace, highly educated and possess a multitude of skills. Their life expectancy is just over 100 years.

The Gracians consider themselves equal to one another regardless of intelligence, education, or occupation, i.e., the person who farms the land or who drives a local transportation vehicle or who directs a hospital has the same social status. This includes respect, appreciation, and understanding of the work everyone performs. From time to time, differences do occur between members of the population. However, they are promptly handled by a panel of arbitrators, usually local, who settle issues with concession and compromise for it is in the Gracians nature to be conciliatory and supportive of a peaceful coexistence.

The Gracians do not worship any gods or higher powers. They did not choose to be atheist. The concept of God or a higher being never entered into their evolution. The start of their civilization has always been a puzzle to them. Despite their high degree of learning and intellect, the Gracians have never been able to explain how they came into being.

They have seen evolutions from primates or aquatic life forms on other planets but there is no evidence of this occurring on planet Grace. Other theories have been pursued but for various reasons, they have been rejected. The most popular and reasonable explanation, as far as the Gracians are concerned, is that beginning settlers were transported to the planet from another world (planet) by a people who were desperately trying to save their race from extinction. Like the other theories there is little evidence to support this belief. But as the Gracians say, they had to start somewhere, and the lack of evolutionary evidence seems to indicate that they came from afar.

Planet Grace is controlled by 400 of its citizens. The group is known as the 'Center' and the individual members are referred to as 'Directors'. This is how the group is organized:

The Center Organization

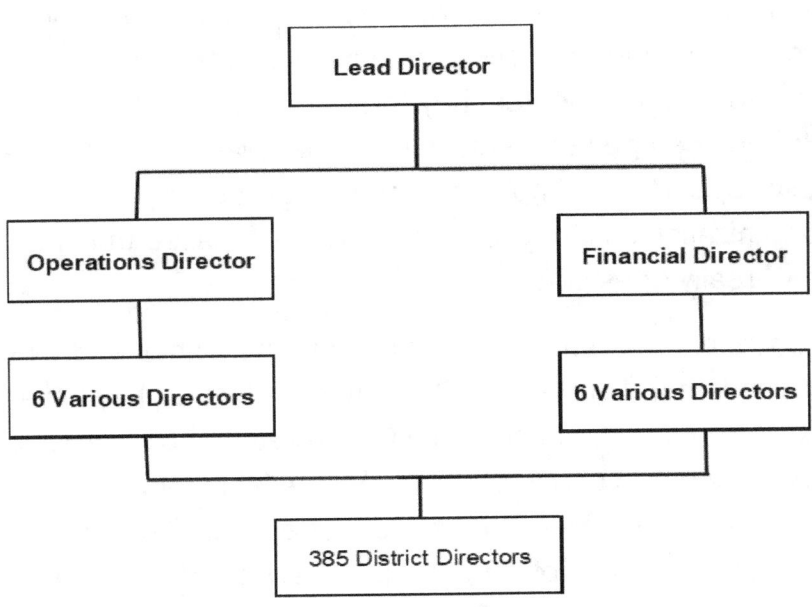

The Center directs the work of tens of thousands of Gracians known as the Work Force. The Work Force is specifically charged with carrying out the Work Directives of the Center. Work Directives are developed based on input from all Gracians. Suggestions for development of Work Directives can flow upward from the Gracian citizenry or downward from the Director group. But in either case, any suggested Work Directive must be approved by a 65% majority of all Gracians over the age of 21 years. Each Gracian gets one vote. All Gracians vote. They see it as their civic duty and are happy to comply. Voting is conducted quarterly and is done electronically from each household. It is strictly controlled.

A unique feature of the Director Group is they can only come from the Work Force and after having served their single six-year term in the Center, they return to the Work Force. Having seen governments fail on other planets, the Gracian's fully support this simple structure of 'Leadership Organization', as they refer to it and are pleased that their 'say' really does count.

Robots are also employed throughout the planet, and they are an integral part of the Gracian labor force. They have no say in running the Leadership Organization. Actually, robots are considered sophisticated, highly reliable tools. The Gracians were careful in their robot development programs because they did not want them to start thinking on their own and become a factor in Gracian society.

Chapter 18

LRGEV167
(Long Range Galaxy Explorer Vehicle 167)

LRGEV167 is a large space craft measuring over 1,500 feet in length, and about 450 feet in diameter. Its design is functional. It is powered by four fusion accelerators and can use a time warp speed system that is similar to time travel. The Gracians developed this system about a century ago and it has enabled them to conduct their far-lung and extensive space explorations

LRGEV167 is 'parked' about 567,000 miles above earth. The medical staff on board is laboring to save the lives of the three astronauts. They are an incredibly talented and dedicated group each having the Earth equivalent of advanced medical degrees. Most have two other advanced degrees, usually Pharmacology and Biology. The Pulmonologist treating the astronauts have these credentials plus master's degrees in some form of space technology. The vehicle's operating staff are also well educated and have skills in multiple areas of space technology and exploration. In summary, the Gracians are very intelligent people. On an Earth I.Q. Scale, they would be in the 500 to 650 range.

Physical examination has shown that all three astronauts are resting comfortably with organs and skeletal systems function well. Overall, they are in good physical condition. The concern is brain and cerebral conditions, more specifically, has oxygen deprivation caused any damage to these delicate, complex parts of their bodies? Their best treatment hope is Micro-Oxygen Infusion. The Gracians started this treatment as soon as they arrived at the drifting ISS module, and it is continuing. The three astronauts are making progress. They have yet to regain consciousness, but their life signs are improving, and brain wave activity has increased. Recovery from oxygen deprivation and hypothermia is a slow, methodical process and the Gracians are being very cautious with the pace of recovery.

The Gracians plan is to bring the astronauts back to full recovery and then deliver them back to Earth. A few of the LRGEV167 crew anticipate contact with the people of Earth so they are studying English as they see it as the most used language on the planet. It has taken the Gracians three days to master the fundamentals of a language they see as inefficient and at times outright puzzling. For example, they see, 'f**k' as a great word with lots of utility that can be used for many parts of speech, but it is socially unacceptable to say or write the word. There are other words in this same 'taboo' category. The Gracians think: why have a word if you can't use it?

Based on their observations, the Gracians feel that the Americans seem to be the lead people on the planet, therefore, they have been studying their culture as well. Again, the inefficiencies are evident, particularly when it comes to getting things done.

The crew of LRGEV167 is of comprised of 75 Gracians, both men and women. There is also a small complement of university co-eds who are serving as interns and apprentices as part of their scholastic development.

To help with the craft's operation, the Gracians also have on board about 50 life-like robots. These robots mirror the size and appearance of the Gracians and would fool the most ardent observer into thinking they were human. They are both male and female but in appearance only. They help with ship operations and maintenance. They also manage the cooking and carry out domestic chores. The robots are highly intelligent and have been programed with a number of skills.

Meanwhile, LRGEV167 is being maneuvered closer to Earth, but the Gracians want to remain undetected until they, and the astronauts, are ready for their Earth landing. They have not yet determined a landing site but given what they have observed about the Earthling's propensity for curiosity, and the aggressive nature of the Earth's media, they have decided to try and land at some type of military base with medium to high security. The vehicle flight crews are already listening in on Earth's air communication in order to have an idea of landing protocols.

Chapter 20

Back on Earth

Back in Houston life is slowly returning to normal, or what is really a new normal, for the three astronaut families. Memorial services are over, the children are back in school and the difficulty of settling into life without a cherished loved one, especially one so integral to the family unit, has started, with remorse and sorrow still on every family member's mind. The kindness shown to the three families by so many individuals and groups was extraordinary and very much appreciated. This is clearly an excellent example of the thoughtful, caring side of the people of Earth.

The NASA folks are just starting their review of the elements of this 'perfect storm' of a tragedy. Why wasn't there any 'back up' shuttle available? Why wasn't the cosmic storm detected sooner? What was the new, previously unknown material that virtually destroyed the ISS? And the larger question: Should the ISS be replaced, or can its function be carried out by other, more up-to-date space platforms?

Another question that should be asked is: Is it time to develop a unified, coordinated program for Earth's space exploration programs? Presently there are several groups that are going off in different directions: exploration, scientific, commercial, and even military. We see one group trying to land on the moon, others are out trying to land on different planets while others are peppering the sky with communication, spy and entertainment satellites. It seems that a collaborative effort is needed. If nothing else, it would take advantage of the economies of shared resources and costs. However, before this can happen, a great deal of other cooperative efforts must take place. But it is good to hope.

The press, of course, is keeping the story alive as it continues to make money selling airtime and other media advertising. Finger pointing, second guessing, conspiracy theories and misinformation abound. Factual reporting is also being aired however, it is hard to tell what is fact and what is fiction. This story will probably continue until some other major event takes its place. Unfortunately, that will only change the subject, not the practice.

Chapter 21

Homeward Bound

Twelve days have passed since the rescue and the condition of the three astronauts continues to improve. They are in an induced semi-conscious state. Captain Frank and Gloria Fan are starting to realize that they are in some type of medical facility, but they also feel that they are in some form of a dream-like state. The attending medical personnel appear normal and attentive. Rakib is still unconscious, but his prognosis is very good, and his mental and physical signs are excellent.

Captain Frank and Gloria were told that they were suffering from asphyxia and hypothermia. They have been advised that their space station has been destroyed by a rogue cosmic cloud. Their dream- like state has prohibited them from asking many questions. They did ask where they were and were told they were in a faraway medical facility.

After several more days of treatment, the LRGEV167 medical staff has decided that the astronauts are well enough to travel back to earth. Rakib's progress is still lagging but he continues to do well and has now progressed to a semi-conscious state. All three astronauts have been aboard the spaceship for 15 days.

Commander Akar Bou (his name, a loose translation from Gracian to English) is in charge of LRGEV167. He has identified about a dozen or so of his officers as personnel who will most likely interact with the Earthlings. In order to simplify identifications, Commander Bou has ordered the ten to take on American names. He will do the same. His name will be Thomas George. He will also make certain that the officers will be fluent in the Americanized version of the English language. Four members of the medical staff have also learned English. They are the most likely Gracians to have an actual working relationship with their counterparts on Earth as they handle the patient turnover. Having members of the Command and Control crew speak fluent English will facilitate clear and concise communications between their ship and the Earth based air traffic controllers and landing personnel.

Commander George would like the astronaut hand off to go as quickly and discreetly as possible. He feels an American military base with its high security systems would be an excellent choice to land his ship. He is also looking for a base with good medical facilities either on-base or in close proximity. He has found three bases that he thinks will fill the bill.

LRGEV167 has an excellent stealth capacity and has far more advanced defenses than America's military has ever seen. It will be easy to arrive at a landing site before visual contact is made. Commander George will use the ship's systems to aid in his desire for discretion. A night landing is also desired.

LRGEV167 has been steadily moving towards Earth and is now about 500 miles off the equatorial region of the planet. The navigators aboard have at least two protocols they must follow. First, they must ask for, and receive, permission to land at the chosen military base which includes identifying who they are and what type of craft they are flying. LRGEV167 will identify itself as an 'experimental' craft with three injured personnel on board in need of medical assistance. Commander George hopes this will satisfy the 'who' and 'what' questions.

Once on landing approach the crew must also seek permission to join a landing pattern. Again, questions will be asked, and the 'experimental craft' answer will be given. Commander George knows this landing plan is not perfect but given the time constraints and the need to get the astronauts home it is the best he has developed. He hopes he is not naive in his thinking.

The ship is made ready for the landing and the 'initial earth contact crew' has modified their uniforms to look more American. Actually, they look somewhat akin to a flight crew from a commercial airliner. The first installation on the Commander's list is Edwards Air Force Base, located in the western portion of the Mojave Desert, about 100 miles northeast of Los Angeles. Edwards AFB radio control tower frequency is acquired. It is 11:00 PM and the first call to the base is initiated.

"Edwards AFB, Edwards AFB this is Experimental Craft LRGEV167. Do you copy?"

The call is repeated twice more but there is no reply. The air traffic controllers at Edwards do, in fact, hear the call but believe it is another in a series of prank calls they receive on an almost daily basis. They choose not to answer.

"Edwards AFB, Edwards AFB this is Experimental Craft LRGEV167. We have three personnel on board that need medical assistance. Do you copy?"

The call is repeated two more times.

The Edwards controllers are now starting to think that there may be something to this transmission. They decide to reply.

"Experimental Craft LRGEV167, this is Edwards AFB. Is your medical situation an emergency?"

"No, it is not. We need a place to land our craft in order get these folks to a hospital ASAP."

"Sir, Edwards AFB is a military installation, and we cannot give landing permission to non-military aircraft. We suggest you consider landing at Palmdale Regional Airport which is in close proximity to Edwards."

"Edwards, we really need a secure place to land, and a municipal airport won't do."

"Sorry LRGEV167 we have our rules and our orders. Palmdale is available and there is a hospital within one mile of the airport. If you need medical attention, please follow our advice, and use Palmdale. We wish you well and good luck. Edwards AFB over and out."

Commander George was not completely surprised by the 'reception' he received at Edwards AFB. The very security he was looking for turned against him. He still has not given up on military bases. His next try will be Lakehurst Naval Air Station, located in the Pine Barrens of southeastern New Jersey. Back in the 1930's Lakehurst NAS was a major base for dirigibles, air ships and blimps. It was also the site of the May 1937 German air ship "Hindenburg" accident which killed 36 people and marked an abrupt end to air ship travel. The hangers that housed these giants of the sky are still standing today.

Commander George will change his message for the Lakehurst air traffic controller without actually mentioning the true nature of his request for a landing. For who would believe he and his crew are actually here to drop off the three astronauts they saved and who were reportedly killed in the ISS debacle.

LRGEV167 has made the trip from Edwards on the west coast to Lakehurst in 37 minutes and is now ready to land in New Jersey.

"Mayday, Mayday, Lakehurst NAS this is Experimental Craft. Do you copy?"

Adding "Mayday" to the call was a mistake. Not only did it get the attention of Lakehurst, but McGuire AFB, 20 miles to the south, Newark and Philadelphia commercial airports, and Northeast Regional Air traffic control are now all on alert. Commercial air traffic in the Northeast Corridor is also monitoring the message.

"LRGEV167, LRGEV167, this Lakehurst Navel Air, what is your emergency?"

"Lakehurst, from LRGEV167. We have three personnel on board that need pulmonary medical assistance. We need to get them to Deborah Heart and Lung Center in Browns Mills. New Jersey"

"LRGEV167 what type of craft are you flying? Is your transponder turned off? We are not getting any signal. And most important, is your aircraft in any danger? Do you have any mechanical issues?"

"We have no mechanical issues. Our craft is operating just fine. We do not have a transponder, and our craft is actually a space cruiser."

That last statement did it. The call from LRGEV167 was immediately recognized as a prank and further transmission from the ground were terminated.

Commander George realizes that this means of communication with Earth is not working and will probably never work. The true reason they are trying to land is just too implausible for anyone on Earth to believe and Commander George understands that. Another approach is needed. After giving this matter some additional thought and reviewing how things work on Earth he develops a new plan. Before he finishes his thought process, he is interrupted by one of his flight officers.

"Sir, the flight group has been reviewing power requirements and the additional fuel needed to conduct an actual landing on Earth. Fuel should be adequate, but we may have to use some of our reserve supplies to get us back home. Our advice is that we should not linger on Earth any more than necessary. This all has to do with the gravity situation we will encounter.

Gracian space explorations are well planned and include safety margins for consumables, such as supplies, and fuel. However, the planning takes place before a mission commences. Provisions for certain known situations and allowances for unplanned circumstances are factored in. Gravity is one of the chief variables. For example, if a mission requires landing on a planet with gravity, which some do, or

118

skirting an area influenced by the gravitational 'pull' of say a moon or a Black Hole, extra fuel may be required.

In the case of this trip, LRGEV167 was not expected to land anywhere, so fuel supplies were calculated accordingly. The extra fuel needed for an Earth landing is not a problem, but it may mean using some of the ship's fuel reserves. This is something the crew prefers not to do.

The Gracians space exploration programs have gone on for thousands of years. They have ranged far and wide. The further the Gracians travel into space the more they realize the limitless nature of the Universe. Their travels have also led to the discovery of 9 life sustaining planets both in and beyond the Milky Way.

Two such planets have only animals living on them. Both have established food chains, water, and oxygen. Minerals have also been found but they are of no use to the Gracians because of the logistics involved getting them back to their planet. On one of these planets a Gracians crew, while out exploring, was attacked by a herd of large, lizard like reptiles. Three of the crew perished and three others were severely wounded.

Six of the other planets contain human forms of life in various stages of evolution from Australopithecus Boisei to Homo Erectus, to early Homo Sapiens. Most of these species viewed the advanced Gracians as coming from the sky, the products of thunder or lighting. These early planet dwellers showed no animosity towards the Gracians, and their common reactions was that of fear, curiosity and wonderment.

Having observed the general warlike nature of the inhabitants of Earth, the Gracians made only cautiously limited contact with small groups of its inhabitants. Now that was about to change.

Commander George decides to make another contact with Earth. If it fails, he will deposit the three astronauts at a safe and convenient place on earth and will include instructions detailing their rescue and their return to Earth.

Commander George's plan to attempt to contact is a simple one. Using the advanced communication system aboard LRGEV167, he will cell phone the person in charge of NASA. He has found that person to be Mr. Ernesto Sosa who is located in Houston, Texas, USA. This makes sense to Commander George because the astronauts work for NASA, and their logo is affixed to the astronaut's uniforms.

Chapter 22

The Phone Call

❝ Good Afternoon, this is the National Aeronautics and Space Administration. How may I direct your call?"

"I would like to talk Director Ernesto Sosa."

"Director Sosa's office, Ann Maloch speaking."

Ann Maloch is a 54 year old divorced grandmother who lives by herself. Her only son and her two grandchildren live in Key West, Florida where he runs a charter boat business. She has worked 36 years for NASA. Her current job is Administrative Assistant to the Director. Ann is smart, feisty and, some say, the real brains behind NASA's administration. And no one gets to see or talk to her boss, Director Sosa, without going through her.

"Ann, please don't hang up. This is not a prank call. This is Commander Thomas George, and I am in charge of the Long Range Galaxy Explorer Vehicle 167. We are orbiting hundreds of miles above the earth. What I am going to tell you next involves the fate of the three ISS astronauts, but first let me ask you, how am I doing so far?

"Your story is farfetched, but you caught me on a slow day, so I want to hear more."

"Great! About two weeks ago we were returning to our home on Planet, Grace."

"You're from another planet"?

"Yes, but that's not relevant right now. Our route took us past Earth. When we got close we heard a stressful conversation between the drifting astronauts and a place called mission control.

We learned that the drifting astronauts were in a dire situation, and we decided to help. A rescue group was dispatched from our ship to their location. They were found near death and were taken back to our ship for medical treatment. They have been recovering and are now healthy enough to return to Earth."

"That's an interesting story but shame on you for building it around people who gave their lives in the name of science and space exploration. Don't bother to call . . . . . ."

"Please wait, I have proof. And please know that I would never disparage the memory of a deceased person, especially one who has so recently passed."

"What kind of proof do you have?"

"I have video of all three astronauts recovering from their ordeal. I can send it to you."

"How do I know the video is not a fake?"

"You can judge for yourself. I just need a cell phone number to send it to."

"I knew there was a catch."

"There is no catch. What am I going to do with a cell phone number?

"I still think it's too weird to be true."

"Watch the video and then you can decide."

"OK, here's the number."

"OK, got it, now here's the video."

Ann watched the video three times. She is still not convinced, but something is telling her that this story could be true. Still, she is skeptical. If only there was more proof, more evidence. She ponders her next move.

"Ok, I watched the video and the three people sort of resemble the astronauts but it's hard to tell."

"Do you think you could approach your boss, Mr. Sosa about this or perhaps put me through to him so I could speak to him?"

"No Way! He'll think I'm crazy if I talk to him about this, and if I put you through to him with this tale, he'll give me hell!"

"Well, what can I do? I can't just carry the astronauts around in our Galaxy Explorer."

"Why don't you just swoop down to Houston, drop them off at the nearest hospital and then fly off to your home planet. Grace, I think you called it."

"You know that's not a bad idea! I am concerned about the chaos that bringing a large spacecraft into the Houston area would create. The people, the press, the traffic. It would be crazy. Are there any landing spots near the hospitals?"

"Yes, Houston is a big metropolis, and most hospitals have helicopter landing pads on their roofs. How big is your spaceship?"

"In American measurements it is 1,200 feet long by 230 feet wide by 74 feet in height or about 4 football fields long and almost half football fields wide."

"Well that certainly won't fit on the roof of hospital landing pad. Can it hover?"

"Yes"

"Well, we have a very large employee parking lot behind our building. You can just hover over it and drop off the three astronauts and blast out of here. We can then ferry them to the hospital by local ambulance."

"That might work but our medical people will have to brief the attending physicians at the hospital so we will have to hang around for a while. Can we talk more about the details of the drop off?"

"You're serious! You really want me to help you plan the drop off! I'm not even convinced that this is real."

"Look you have got to help me. My only other option is to drop them off anyway and I'd rather have some orderly plan to do it. Besides, you don't even need to be involved, just tell me what I need to do, and I'll take care of the rest. We can do it early in the morning when no one is around."

Ann thinks again. Her only involvement will be to help prepare a plan for a large spaceship to visit Houston for a short period and drop off three rescued astronauts, in need of medical assistance, and arrange for transportation to a local hospital. What could go wrong? Everything!

But Ann decides to help anyway. Ann and Commander Thomas spend the next 45 minutes on the phone going over the details of this improbable exercise. Ann has dictated what needs to be done. Twice she changed her mind about helping only to have Commander Thomas talk her out of it. In the end, the plan is finalized, and Ann does have several tasks to perform. But most of her involvement happens after the ship's arrival is reported so there will be no appearance of pre-involvement on her part. The only thing she needs to do in advance is to get the support of the Houston Police Department, and she has a plan for that.

Clarence Brown is a 28 year veteran with the Houston Police Department. He holds the rank of Captain and is a trained Incident Commander whose specialty is 'crowd control'. Captain Brown is the guy who runs the Mobile Incident Command Center and who directs the squads of police to maintain law and order during crowd involved incidents.

Clarence Brown has attended St. Leo the Great Church for the past 21 years where he sings in the choir with Ann Maloch, a 24 year member of the church. They also work together supporting other church activities.

Ann calls Clarence and after some social chit-chat delicately starts to describe the plan for the spaceship landing. Clarence is polite enough not to interrupt her. When she is finished, he sits back and tries to make sense of what he has just heard.

"Ann, I have known you for twenty years. You have always been a sane rational person, not given to flights of fantasy, but this, I just don't know what to say. This is obviously some prank, but why do you believe it?"

"I just have a feeling and I'm really not going to participate in the actual event. I am just going to maybe go to NASA headquarters at the designated time of arrival and see what happens. I'm calling you just to tell you about it and ask if you are in the area that you stand by just in case you are needed. I mean I don't, want the spaceship to land and then occupants come out and the police start shooting at them. You also may be needed for crowd control."

"By 'occupants' do you mean the aliens?"

'Yes"

"Do you know how ridiculous that sounds? When is this supposed to happen anyway?"

"6:00 AM Tomorrow"

In the end Ann's powers of persuasion win out and Clarence agrees to be in the area of NASA Headquarters at the designated time. He claims to have business in that area tomorrow morning anyway.

Chapter 23

Landing in Houston

It is 5:00 AM the next day and LRGEV167 is about to make its rapid 500 mile descent to Earth. They call Gulf Coast Regional Air Traffic Control to alert them about their descent into the Houston area. They no longer ask permission because no one believes them anyway. In this case their call is rebuffed, and they are warned about the heavy fines and jail penalties for using commercial air traffic radio frequencies for prank calls.

Commander George sees there are three commercial airliners in proximity to their intended landing area. They are not close enough to be in any danger, but he figures it's best to at least warn them that they may see some unusual vertical flight activity.

"American 206, Delta 98 and United 8162, this is Long Range Galaxy Explorer Vehicle 167. This is a courtesy call to let you know that we will be making a vertical landing in the vicinity of NASA Headquarters, Houston, in about 3 minutes.

You are not in any danger, but you may see some unusual lighting displays. There is no need to change your flight paths. Again, you are far enough away and in no immediate danger."

"This is Houston Regional Air Traffic Control. We are ordering you to get off this radio frequency immediately!"

At about 15,000 feet, LRGEV167 activates its landing lights which cast about as much light as an NFL football stadium. The three commercial airliners are awed by the sight and are very happy to have gotten advanced warning. Ann Maloch has been parked in the NASA visitors parking lot since 5:00 AM. She is amazed at what she sees and also relieved that she was not a victim of someone's practical joke. Her gut told her that the Space Commander's story was true, and it was. Captain Brown is also witnessing the lights from his vantage point about three miles from NASA Headquarters. He too is astonished at what he sees. He can also see the outline of a very large spacecraft. He calls Ann Maloch,

"Are you seeing this?"

"Yes, I am. I am here in the parking lot of NASA Headquarters. Now don't go to try to arrest or shoot at them. They are friendly people!"

In a matter of minutes Houston area towns and municipalities are flooded with 911 calls. SWAT teams and squads of police, fire and emergency responders are sent to the area of

NASA headquarters. The National Guard is put on alert and NORAD jet fighters have been scrambled from Fort Worth AFB

LRGEV167 is now hovering about 75 feet above the NASA parking lot. This is quite a sight! At least 50 police and emergency response vehicles have surrounded NASA Headquarters. They are all keeping a safe distance. News helicopters are darting in and out of the area, and military aircraft are making surveillance passes. And both Houston's airports have ordered ground stops. Thousands of curiosity seekers are starting to flood the area, and some people are actually fleeing the chaotic scene.

This is exactly what Commander Thomas was trying to avoid. He is looking for the three ambulances that were supposed to take the astronauts to Methodist Hospital. Instead, there are thirty. One good thing is that crowds and the emergency responders are all being held at the outer perimeter of the NASA complex.

It is now one hour since the landing (hovering). Captain Brown has set up an Incident Command Post and he has taken charge of the Police, Fire and EMT responders. Also present at the Post are local politicians, and military and federal agency personnel. Right now, the order is to 'stand down and await further instructions.

Commander Thomas has decided to ask whoever is in charge for help in getting the astronauts to the hospital. He does not know how to go about this, so he decides to call Ann Maloch and seek her advice.

"Ann, this is Commander Thomas from the 'Spaceship'. I guess you know by now we have landed. I need your help. I have to get the astronauts to the hospital. I don't know where the ambulances are, and I don't see how they can get through this chaos."

"It is a frantic scene, but I know two people who can help. Would you be willing to meet with them?"

"Why yes, of course. Where would this meeting take place"?

"In the parking lot right near your spacecraft, and I think my one friend will keep the crowds from intruding. I will call as soon as I set it up."

Ann's first call is to Captain Brown. He is an easy sell because he knows she has a legitimate connection with the spaceship's personnel. She warns Captain Brown about discretion because the three astronaut families are not aware that their three loved ones have been rescued and are alive. He agrees to the meeting.

The harder sell will be her boss, NASA Director Ernesto Sosa. She makes the call and is happy to hear he is close by in the vicinity of the Incident Command post.

"Mr. Sosa, this is Ann your secretary. Are you in a place you can talk?

"I am standing next to my car just outside the incident Command Center near the NASA building."

"Good. Get in your car."

"OK what's up?"

"I am in the NASA Visitors parking lot very near the spaceship. I am going to tell you something that you won't believe but just keep listening anyway.

I found out yesterday that the spaceship was coming here to Houston. The spaceship Commander contacted me. Actually, he called you, but there was no way I was putting the call through. After a lengthy conversation I was convinced that the call was legitimate, and I agreed to help him with his mission. That is why I am here now; I am waiting to meet with him. Now this is the really important part, the spaceship crew rescued our three ISS astronauts as they rapidly drifted away from Earth. The astronauts are alive! They were near death and have been undergoing treatment in the spaceship's medical facility for the last two weeks. They are now well enough to continue their medical treatment here on Earth. The Commander's mission is to return the astronauts to Earth and deliver them to a local hospital. I suggested Methodist hospital.

We have to let the astronaut's families know that they are alive. That's where you come in. Obviously, this is a very delicate matter. We have to develop a plan to conduct the notifications and there are some logistics involved. First, we have to verify that the astronauts are here and that they are alive. Then we can notify the families and then we can move the astronauts to the hospital. We have to avoid any information leaks because we do not want the astronaut families to learn they are alive from some TV newscast. As of right now there are only three people that know the astronauts are alive; you and I and a friend of mine, Captain Brown of the Houston Police Department. What do you think?"

"I want to think you're crazy, but I know you're not. I have a thousand question, plus this whole story defies belief, and I cannot believe you are doing all of this without even seeing the astronauts. But I am going to jump over all of that and ask; what do you want me to do?"

"It is simple. Captain Brown will pick you up, he's running the incident Command post. You two will meet me in the parking lot and we will all meet Commander Thomas from the spaceship. We will then develop a plan to get the three astronauts to the hospital and to notify their families that they are alive.

Chapter 24

Meeting The Aliens

Captain Brown and Director Sosa meet Ann in the parking lot near what appears to be the front end of the spaceship. Ann had set up this location as a meeting place. As soon as they arrive, steam like vapors emanate from the underside of the ship, followed by a hissing sound. Two figures descend, seemingly in mid-air. They reach the ground and walk towards the three Earthlings.

"I am Commander Thomas George, and this is my assistant Carol Floy. You must be Mrs. Maloch."

"I am. Please call me Ann. And these two gentlemen are, NASA Director Ernesto Sosa and Captain Clarence Brown from the Houston Police Department."

Cordial handshakes go all around, and Director Sosa offers his profound thanks on behalf of NASA and the American people for rescuing the astronauts. Aliens meeting Earthlings! The scene is surreal. Director Sosa then asks.

"When can we see our astronauts?"

"We will bring them from the ship as soon as the three ambulances arrive. They will be a little groggy, but you can talk to them if you wish."

Ann interrupts and explains that the three astronaut's families have not yet been told that their loved ones have been rescued and until that happens everything must be done with complete discretion.

The plan is discussed. Commander George suggested that two of his medical personnel travel with the astronauts to the hospital so they can review the medical condition and treatment status of the astronauts with hospital personnel. Director Sosa is a close friend of the hospital director, and he agrees to call him in advance and advise him of the situation. He will also travel to the hospital to answer any questions and help with the patient transfer. Ann has agreed to make the phone calls to the astronaut's families. Captain Brown suggested that he manage the transport of the families to the hospital. Given the chaotic traffic situation and the state of mind the families will be in, he does not think it wise that they drive themselves to the hospital.

Captain Brown calls for the three ambulances and four police cars. Commander Thomas readies the astronauts for ship alighting. Ann and Director Sosa will wait until they actually see the astronauts before they make their calls, despite everything that's happened, seeing is believing.

The ambulances arrive and Captain Brown's men commandeer them, collect cell phones, and shut off vehicle radios. He briefs the ambulance crews on the need for secrecy.

Once again, steam like vapors emanate from the underside of the ship, followed by the hissing sound. Two figures and a gurney descend and just like that, Captain Hammel, is back to earth. Ann and Director Sosa move to the gurney and squeeze the captain's hand. He replies, looks up at them and smiles. He is quickly loaded into the ambulance.

This act is repeated two more times, and all three astronauts are back on earth. Rakib Rajbir appears to have some medical apparatus attached to him and Commander Thomas explains that his recovery is not quite as far along as the other two astronauts, but his recovery is progressing nicely.

Ann decides that since she has police cars at her disposal, she will give the good news to the families in person. The first stop is Captain Hammel's house. She arrives with the police in tow. Patty Hammel answer the door. Just last week NASA officially declared that her husband was killed in the ISS mishap, what else could it be. She is not even aware of the spaceship's arrival. She recognizes Ann, from NASA.

"Patty, good morning. I have astoundingly good news for you. Frank is alive! And he is here in Houston!"

Patty's knees give out and she starts to sink to the floor only to be steadied by a Houston Police Officer.

"How is this possible? When did you find out about this? Are you sure it's him? I thought he was a million miles out in space."

"We're sure. I saw him with my own eyes!"

Ann hurriedly tells Patty of the details.

"Patty, we are here to take you to the hospital right now so you can be with him. Are the children home?"

"No, they are at school."

"Great we will pick them up along the way."

The stop at the school was interesting to say the least. The children were taken out of class and escorted to the principal's office. There, Patty tells them the news, after a moment of disbelief followed by tears of joy, the two children and Patty speed away to the hospital leaving the entire school abuzz. Ann left in a second police car and was on her way to Rakib Rajbir's home.

"Asha Rajbir, I am Ann Maloch from NASA."

"Yes, I know who you are."

"I have some incredible news for you. Rakib is alive!"

Ann tells them the story. What followed is an incredible happy scene with Asha's parents joining in the celebration. They cannot believe what they are hearing, and they are most anxious to see Rakib.

"The children! The children! We must get the children!" Exclaims Asha. She wants to drive and pick them up right away, but Ann explains why it is better for the police to do the driving.

So off they all go to the school and then off to the hospital.

Ann is traveling to her final stop, Gloria Fan's home. Mr. and Mrs. Fan have been watching the news and listening to all of the media's speculation about the spaceship but nowhere was the astronauts' rescue and their return to earth mentioned.

Ann delivers her joyous message, and the Fans express their happiness and thank Ann for bringing such good news to the house. Tears of joy show on both of their faces. They are eager to see their daughter and happily accept the police's offer for a ride to the hospital. Ann travels with them.

Chapter 25

Reunion

The scene at the hospital is frenzied and chaotic. Reporters have followed the three ambulances from the spaceship to the hospital and have set up shop *en masse* just outside of the hospital perimeter. The arrival of the first two police cars with civilian passengers stirs up the crowd even more and adds a new element to their speculative reporting.

NASA Director Sosa arrived earlier and along with the hospital director has arranged for a special section in the ICU to be set up for the three astronauts and their families.

The hospital has also put together a special group of 'Astronaut Doctors' to handle any needed treatment for the three astronauts. They call themselves the 'astro docs'. What they were not expecting was that the three patients would be accompanied by two medical personnel from the spaceship itself. At first, they appear like normal personnel but soon it becomes evident that their training and medical techniques are far more advanced than those of the astro docs.

Nevertheless, they make it clear they are only here to advise and not to take charge.

The hospital staff refers to them as the 'space docs.' They explain that Ms. Fan and Captain Hammel are no longer in need of much treatment and that their organs and brains just need time to continue to oxygenize themselves. They believe that this process or healing should take 4-5 more days.

Mr. Rajbir Is another story. The space docs say that he was very near to being clinically dead. He was more oxygen deprived than the other two. They were able to bring him around, but his full recovery will take at least 10 days, and he is still being treated with the help of pulmonary and oxygenation equipment. They do expect him to make a full recovery.

The three astronauts are immediately placed in quarantine which is normal for astronauts returning from a space mission. Quarantine testing should take about 48 hours. However, family members will be able to see and talk to them right away.

The Hammels are first to arrive at the hospital. They are taken to the ICU where a very emotional reunion takes place in spite of the glass quarantine enclosure that separates them from their husband and father. The family just keeps saying, "we just can't believe it."

The reunion with Gloria Fan and her parents went equally well. Mr. Fan expresses his concern about his daughter's appearance, which is understandably pale and thin, but she jokes back that it is nothing some bowls of rice won't fix. He has taken a number of pictures including a selfie through the glass and sent them to friends and relatives in San Diego and Taiwan. The Fans express their sincere thanks and gratitude to all those who brought about this happy moment. Mr. Fan asked if NASA could arrange a meeting, if possible, with the people in charge of the spaceship so he may thank them personally. All and all, it is a happy moment for Wu and Chi-Ling Fang.

Rakib Rajbir's meeting is slightly different from his fellow astronauts. For one thing he is barely conscious. He is also connected to several strange looking pieces of medical apparatus. This makes his appearance a little frightening. However, the medical staff, including a member of the LRGEV167 medical unit are quick to assure his family that Rakib is in good medical condition and that they expect him to make a full recovery. They go on to explain why his recovery is lagging behind the other astronauts and that several days ago they were in the same stage of recovery that Rakib is in now.

Chapter 26

Extra, Extra, Read All About it!

A press conference is scheduled for 11:00 AM and it promises to be a media circus. Speakers will include Director Sosa, Hospital Director Dr. Earl Berman, and Commander George Thomas of the Space Craft LRGEV167. Ann Maloch was also present on the dais along with some politicians, but none of them are scheduled to speak. The fact that Commander Thomas was going to speak was a surprise to everyone and certainly increased interest in the conference.

Director Sosa spoke first. He talked about the communication received by NASA from the Space Craft, LRGEV167 and their news of astronaut rescue out in deep space. He explained how the delivery plan was developed and ends by thanking the Commander and crew of the spaceship and the people on the ground who are continuing to help with the astronaut's recovery. He also asks that questions be held until the end of the conference.

Dr. Berman spoke next. He gave a report on the recovery and medical condition of the three astronauts, how they were found by their rescuers in near death condition and how they were rehabilitated aboard the space craft over a period of twelve days. He explained that advanced recovery procedures used by the spaceship's medical personnel were largely responsible for saving the astronauts' lives. He went on to say that without these procedures and techniques the astronauts would not be here today. He closed by saying that the astronauts are in temporary isolation and that they all are expected to make full recoveries.

The final and most anticipated speaker is LRGEV167 Commander Thomas George.

"Good afternoon, ladies, and gentlemen. My name is Thomas George, and I am Commander of the Long Range Galaxy Explorer Vehicle 167 or the 'spaceship' as you Earthlings like to call it."

This garners some laughter from the crowd.

"Waiting my turn to speak, I was trying to decide where to begin. First of all, English is not our language. However, knowing we were going to land on Earth and that some of our crew, including myself, would be interacting with you folks, we decided to learn one of the most popular languages spoken on Earth.

Home to us is a planet called Grace. We are located in the Milky Way Galaxy some 26 light years from Earth. We have escaped detection by Earth's astronomers due to our relative position to your planet and because of the dust and gas fields that populate the Galaxy. Our planet is about the size of earth, we have two suns and there is no axis tilt which makes for only one season. Our day is 21.5 hours with light and dark split evenly.

We Gracians have been aware of your planet for quite some time. In fact, we have visited Earth on four occasions, 1299 BC, 623 BC, 1864 AD and 1943 AD. Our earlier visits may help to explain some of the unusual land and rock formations built or created by the Earth's inhabitants long ago probably after they witnessed our landings.

From an evolutionary standpoint, our civilization is about 5,800 years further along than where Earth is right now. One result is our intellectual level is higher. Using Earth's I. Q. scale, we are in the 500 to 650 Range as compared to your current range of 100 to 150. I mention this purely as a reference and certainly not to prove or boast of any superiority. We have simply been around longer than you have.

Again, more laughter from the crowd

"Our science and technology is much further along than what we see on Earth. This has allowed us to accomplish so much more in the area of space exploration."

Commander George went on to explain what brought them to be passing by Earth at the precise time of the ISS mishap and how they heard the distress calls from the station to earth. He mentioned the comradery Gracian space explorers share with their fellow space travelers especially in times of danger or mishap and their decision to try and help the drifting astronauts. He detailed the rescue mission itself and how they rehabilitated the three astronauts aboard their spacecraft.

Commander Thomas closed his remarks by explaining how difficult it was to try and get permission to land in America and how they wanted to do it with a minimum of fanfare. Again, laughter from the crowd.

It was now time for the question and answer portion of the news conference. Director Sosa and Doctor Berman were both asked questions of a more or less general nature regarding when the astronauts will be released, any lasting effects of their ordeal, what it was like to work with an alien medical team and if the ISS would be rebuilt. In answer to the ISS rebuild question Director Sosa said he would like to see a new station built but it would take world-wide effort, financing, and most important cooperation to get that done.

The questions directed at Commander George were the most anticipated.

"Commander George, when you visited earth, how long did you stay?'

"Our time here usually lasted several weeks which gave us opportunities to make a number of aerial observations.

145

During the earlier visits, we made stops to talk with local inhabitants about their customs, rituals, and practices. Some of the people we met were friendly, some were hostile, and others treated us as gods, offering up women and children as sacrifices or simply to take with us."

"Why didn't you visit more often?"

"The Gracians did not think that Earth had much to offer them. On each visit they observed a planet struggling with development, and almost constant fighting for one cause or another. Planet Earth seemed to harbor a preoccupation with unrest and conflict that centered on religion or land possession."

This answer was met with silence but then the questioning continued.

"Do you worship or believe in god."

"We do not. We are familiar with the concept of worshiping a god or spirit or deity but In our case, it just never entered into our cultural development."

"What is the average life expectancy on your plant? Do all of the people look like you? Where did you come from?"

"The average life expectancy is about 100 years. We are of one race. And we are not 100% certain of our origin. There is no evidence that we evolved from plant or animal life. We believe we were transported to Planet Grace from another planet perhaps in an attempt to save that planet's civilization but there is no empirical evidence to support this. We just don't know for sure."

"Do you have families? Do you marry?"

"Yes to both of those questions"

"How fast does you space vehicle go"

"The propulsion system aboard our ship is very sophisticated and it can achieve 'speeds' beyond the 'speed' of your measurement of light. I say this because our process of travelling through space is different than say, travelling through space on a straight line at a certain velocity. Simply stated our method of travel is different than yours."

"How many people are on board your ship?" And will they be getting off to take a look around?"

"Our crew size is about 75 and we will not be granting any 'shore leave' during this trip. Besides Disney Land is too far away!"

More Laughs from the crowd.

The questioning continued for a while longer, and Director Sosa then called an end to the proceedings.

Chapter 27

Recovery

Five days have passed since the landing. Captain Hammel and Gloria Fan have been released from the hospital and are at home with their families. Rakib Rajbir is fully conscious and is scheduled to be released in a day or so. The prognosis for all three astronauts is excellent. They are expected to make full recoveries and are not expected to suffer any long term affects from their near death experience with the ISS calamity. The two medical staff members from LRGEV167 have returned to their ship. They received numerous accolades from the astronauts, hospital medical staff, NASA and even the president of the United States for their help with the astronauts' recovery.

The folks at NASA are continuing with their investigation of the ISS incident. The press has eased up on their criticism of the Agency and public attention has shifted to more current news items. Director Sosa and his team have also started to work on a study that addresses the future of the ISS. NASA has taken the lead on this project which promises to be no easy task. Decision number one is whether or not the ISS

should be replaced. This will require worldwide input and cooperation and will be a major challenge in, and of, itself.

Of course, the number one story in the world media is the spaceship. It has moved away from Houston and, actually away from Earth itself, to escape the effects of Earth's gravity. Hovering LRGEV167 over the NASA parking lot or, anywhere else on earth for that matter, was consuming significant amounts of fuel. It is now sitting some 300 miles from the Earth, where it is being readied for the trip back to Planet Grace. News agencies, governments, scientists, and average citizens have all tried to contact the ship for a myriad of reasons, but the ship has refused contact. However, they have taken the time to send polite refusals to the more legitimate requests. After all, they know a thing or two about alien contact and diplomacy.

Chapter 28

LRGEV167 Problem

Commander Thomas is holding a staff meeting with his key officers when the ship's Chief Engineer interrupts the meeting. He expresses his concern about whether the fuel on board will be sufficient to get them back to Planet Grace. He went on to say that the rescue, earth landing, and more than 2 days of hovering over the Houston area have consumed far more fuel than previously calculated. Commander George asks if there are any other concerns with trip preparations. All other meeting participants answer in the negative, and he adjourns the meeting.

Commander George then calls Space Exploration Headquarters (SEH) back on Planet Grace to advise them of the fuel shortage. He explained that the original trip itinerary had no plans for encountering gravitational situations and that the rescue changed all of that. He went on to say that far more power and fuel were required to deal with the gravitational forces encountered by the Earth landing.

SEH said they understood and that they would develop a solution and reply promptly.

About one hour later, they confirmed the fact that the ship did not have enough fuel to reach Plant Grace at the planned speed. Slowing the ship's speed would save fuel but would add considerable time to the journey home.

They see that the best option is to add or increase LRGEV167's fuel inventory. This has been done before with other ships and involves landing on a planet, mining or gathering the raw materials, and processing them into usable fuel. The ship has the equipment on board to do this but finding a planet with the proper resources and a reasonable environment in which to work is another story.

Another fuel source which is close at hand is Depleted Uranium or DU. It is a spent by-product of Uranium-235 (U-235). Uranium-235 has many uses on Earth, including, fuel for nuclear power plants, nuclear weapons, marine propulsion (mostly naval), power supply for weather stations in remote areas, space vehicles, radiation shielding, and as projectiles in armor-piercing weapons. Every year over 50,000 tons of DU join already substantial stockpiles in the USA, Europe, and Russia. World stock is about 1.6 million tons.

DU does contain small percentages of U-235, but it is considered 'spent' as a fuel supply for most nuclear applications. LRGEV167 has the capability to extract these small bits of uranium and to turn them into usable fuel for the spacecraft. SEM suggests contacting the United States

Government and requesting that the crew be allowed to process enough DU, they estimate 25,000 tons, to fulfill their fuel needs.

Commander George agrees to this suggestion. He feels that this request should be quick and easy, for the United States is indebted to the LRGEV167's crew for saving the three astronauts. Reducing their stockpile of DU will also save storage expenses.

He puts a call into NASA Director Sosa.

"Good morning Ann, this Commander Thomas. How are you doing?

"Commander George, it is so good to hear from you. Where are you?

"I'm out in space, about 500 miles from Houston"

"You haven't left the area yet?"

"No, not yet. May I speak to Director Sosa"?

"Ernesto Sosa here. Is this my good friend Commander Thomas?"

"Yes, it is."

"To what do I owe the pleasure of this call?"

"Ernesto, I have a problem that is delaying my departure and I'm hoping you can help me."

Commander George went on to explain his fuel problem and the solution his SEM advisors came up with.

"Ernesto, what I am looking for is the proper way to ask your government for access to the DU material. Who do I call?"

"I can do better than that. I can make some phone calls on your behalf and see If can get you an OK to start the fuel processing. I will call you as soon I have some results."

Director Sosa's first call is to the director of the Nuclear Regulatory Commission (NRC). He explains the situation and is not surprised to hear the commissioner admit that he has no authority to grant such a request and that he would have to get back to him. Director Sosa tells the commissioner that this is a rather urgent matter, and time is of the essence. The commissioner understands but advises that there is nothing further he can do but that he would make some phone calls. He also mentioned the request involved nuclear material and that raised the subject to a much higher level. Director Sosa made some additional phone calls but soon realized that going through the NRC was the proper way to proceed.

Twenty-Four Hours have passed without any word from the NRC. Director Sosa's patience are wearing thin, and he is trying to come up with other ways to move the permission process along. He has made a fast friendship with Commander George, and he does not want to let him down. They have spent some time together during his brief period on Earth and he has developed a deep appreciation for the "man from outer space". Just as he was contemplating his next move, Ann Maloch buzzed him on the intercom to tell him that the White House Chief of Staff was on the phone.

"Director Sosa, this is White House Chief of Staff, Nick Spano. We have been going over your request, or more correctly the spaceship Commander George's request to access to our Depleted Uranium Stockpiles for the purpose of converting some of it to fuel for his spacecraft.

The President is very much in favor of giving permission to access the DU. To quote him directly he said 'Hell, they saved three of our astronauts, the least we can do is give them some fuel to get back to their home planet.' But it is not his approval to give. Since we are talking about nuclear material with potential bomb making capabilities, a situation like this comes under the War Powers Act and must be approved by the Senate and the House of Representatives. We are preparing a request, but Congress is not in session, and this is not an actual threat to our country's safety and well-being. I am afraid it's going to take ten days to two weeks to get the request processed. I am sorry it can't be sooner, but rules are rules."

"Chief Spano, I understand the rule thing, but is there any way around this? After all these folks did save the lives of three of our astronauts."

"Not that we can see, Director Sosa."

"Thank you for the call."

Director Sosa is visibly upset by this latest turn of events. He himself is a bureaucrat. He understands how things can get bogged down in the 'system', but in light of what the Gracian's did for the United States, he can't believe that there is not some way around this red tape. Our government, our bureaucracy, is really failing us.

"Ms. Maloch, please put a call into Commander George"

"Commander George, I'm afraid I don't have good news for you."

Director Sosa goes on to explain the delay in obtaining access to the DU stockpile. He adds that even after the delay, permission may not be granted. Commander Thomas is taken aback by this news. Depleted Uranium is a nuisance material that costs the United States tens of millions of dollars per year to store. He is offering to reduce the stockpile which, in turn would reduce the cost to maintain it. Why wouldn't the government jump at the chance? And to suggest that the crew of LRGEV167 would make Nuclear weapons out of this material is utterly ridiculous. But the worst is that the President of the United States says that he supports the request and would like to help but has no power to do so. This is simply unfathomable to him. Commander Thomas thanks Director Sosa for his efforts and relays this latest turn of events to his superiors back on Planet Grace.

The Gracians and the Commander develop a plan. They will abandon their efforts to deal with the Americans and turn their attention to other countries. Their research tells them that France has 56 nuclear power plants, that produce 63% of their country's electricity. Germany has decided to phase out their Nuclear power generating facilities entirely as of 2023. They did have as many as 35 Nuclear power plants before the phase out. As a consequence, both countries have large stockpiles of Depleted Uranium and both, particularly Germany, are more than willing to rid themselves of as much of the DU they can.

Once again, Commander George takes the lead on this fuel making attempt. Contacts are made, phone calls are made, and the necessary permissions are granted. As part of the deal, the French president asks for a three hour sit down with Commander Thomas simply to discuss the many differences between their two worlds. Germany's chancellor has a similar request, and he would like Commander George to give a full briefing of the uranium extraction process to Germany's chief Nuclear scientists and engineers plus a timetable before any work commences. Commander Thomas agrees and suggests that their French counterparts be invited to the briefing.

Commander George contacts his superiors back on Planet Grace. They are happy to hear of his success in setting up the fuel extracting process. They suggest that as a thank you gesture he set up some help or advice regarding a medical or scientific research project that the Earthlings have been working on.

They also mention their displeasure with the Americans. They were not looking for any pay back for their life saving efforts with the three astronauts, but refusal to allow them to process some unwanted Nuclear waste material is something the Gracians cannot understand. This type of behavior is simply not a part of the Gracian culture.

Chapter 29

Fuel Processing – France

Setting up the Uranium extracting process has begun. It will start in France. LRGEV167 will be moved from its holding station, now 300 mile above the earth to the first of four French DU stockpile depots. The ship will hover in place during the entire processing period. Normally the hovering would consume significant amounts of fuel, however the Gracians have modified the ship so that only a small portion of its propulsion system would be needed to support the extended hovering periods. Additional fuel will be consumed, and that amount will add to the collection volume.

The meeting with Commander Thomas, his technical staff, and the French nuclear scientists and engineers goes well. The French understand the process and although they lack the know-how and equipment to undertake such an extraction, they have learned how the technology works and thanks to the teachings of the LRGEV167 crew, they hope to develop their own process within five years. And most important, they understand the process is safe and that no bombs can be made from the extracted Uranium.

The set-up, processing run time and clean up should take about 10 days to complete. It will consume approximately 85% of France's Depleted Uranium. When finished the yield should be about 4.5 tons of Uranium-235 and 25,000 tons of a benign white powder similar to gypsum. This material can be used as a plaster substitute or as an aggregate used in making cement.

The meeting between the French President and several of his staff and Commander Thomas and several of the LRGEV167 crew, was a huge success. It was very one-sided with the Frenchmen asking question after question. They were simply overwhelmed by what they were learning from their alien visitors. Their questions ran the gamut from what they ate for breakfast, to how the government was run, to the structure of the family, to space travel, and so on. There were many moments of awe during the almost 6 hour visit but the one that the Frenchmen will remember forever is this one: About three-quarters through the meeting, Commander Thomas was explaining how far along the Gracians had come in the field of robotics. He then asked one of his female crew members to take off her hair and her top. She did as requested only to reveal that she was not human at all, just a robot. The Frenchmen, including the President could not believe their eyes. The Commander invited the Frenchmen to touch and feel the robot's arms and face as he pointed out an electronic outlet in the small part of her back that allowed for charging and reprogramming. The Frenchmen were speechless.

"That's why she didn't drink any of the Perrier we put out for her! "Mon Dieu!", exclaimed one of the Frenchman.

The meeting ended on a very high note with Commander Thomas promising to contact the President before he left France.

LRGEV167 is in place over the first DU stockpile and a test of the extraction process is underway. The spaceship's crew are operating the process and collecting the recovered U-235 while French personnel are handling the gypsum-like material. All is going well, and the extracting process is moving along at a faster pace than expected.

Chapter 30

CERN

The European Organization for Nuclear Research, known as CERN, is an intergovernmental organization that operates the largest particle physics laboratory in the world. CERN'S origins can be traced to 1949 when a small number of visionary scientists in Europe and North America identified the need for Europe to have a world class physics research facility. Their vision was to stop the brain drain to America that began during WW II and to provide a force for unity in post-war Europe. CERN was established in 1954; it is based in Meyrin, Switzerland, a western suburb of Geneva, on the France–Switzerland border. It is comprised of twenty-three member states. CERN's mission is to help uncover what the composition of the universe is and how it supports the working of the universe itself.

CERN's main function is to operate particle accelerators and other infrastructure to support high-energy physics research. Since its inception, numerous experiments have been performed at the facility through international collaborations. CERN is the site of a Large Hadron Collider (LHC), the world's largest and highest-energy particle collider. The LHC is a major system in the research work of Particle Acceleration.

CERN provides research services to the world-wide scientific community. As researchers require remote access to this facility, the lab has historically been a major wide area network hub. In developing this hub, CERN gave birth to the World Wide Web as can be seen in most email addresses, i.e. www.

The scientific community on Planet Grace was curious about the research performed at CERN and asked Commander Thomas to have his crew gather some general information about their work. When they heard that CERN was using a Large Hadron Collider (LHC) their attention level was raised.

Hundreds of years ago in the early stages of their particle research period, the Gracians employed an apparatus similar to the Large Hadron Collider used by CERN. For 50 years the collider was a key piece in their research tool arsenal. But then doubts started to arise about data developed by the collider. It turned out the collider operation itself was skewing data output. The culprits were dark forces that were being created as a by-product of the intense collider operation. Worse, skewed data went undetected because when the collider was tested for accuracy and correctness, its software would learn from the test input and generate answers that the test wanted to see. This was truly an authentication nightmare and one that set their research back an undetermined number of years.

There is no doubt that since its inception, CERN has played and will continue to play a significant research role in the fields of medicine, environmental sciences, energy generation and conservation, and general scientific research. The Gracians want to warn the CERN operators of this possible collider operating glitch. They see this warning as a good will gesture among fellow scientific researchers and also as a token of their thanks to France for their help with the LRGEV167's fuel situation.

The Gracians ask Commander Thomas to deliver this information to the CERN representatives and his French contacts in person. The CERN people are delighted and honored to meet with the commander. They are very thankful for his advice which he gives to them in the form of an advanced scientific paper which not only contains detail instructions on finding inherent collider problems but also new research projects that can use collider research assistance.

The French president has left word with his staff that he will be the main contact with anyone from the spaceship. When he hears that the commander has requested a meeting, he is more than happy to oblige. The meeting is arranged. Commander Thomas reports that their fuel recovery project is complete. It has consumed about 84% of France's DU stockpile with an estimated storage cost reduction of € 60 million. He states this is a win for his spaceship and a win for France and he extends his thanks to the country. The French agree about the mutual win for both of them. The Commander than goes on to explain the collider business with CERN and how France's help with the fuel situation played a role in the Gracian's desire to offer a token of their appreciation to an organization of which France is a big part. Finally, the commander offers a personal gift which he hands to the President. The President comments that it is quite heavy. He opens the box and is astounded at what he sees. It is a 62 karat uncut diamond that the Gracian space explorers found on an unnamed, unmanned plant out in the far reaches of the Milky Way Galaxy. The commander goes on to explain that this was found in a desert-like area along with many others. They were simply laying on the surface and were probably created by some unknown force like a high impact crash, or explosion, or perhaps an unknown galactic phenomenon.

Chapter 31

On to Germany

Their fuel gathering mission completed in France, the Gracians, and their good ship, LRGEV167 relocated to Germany to continue their fuel gathering operation. They French operation yielded more fuel than they originally anticipated, and it will provide a higher fuel safety margins.

The start-up of the fuel operation in Germany will be quicker than in France because of the meetings and planning conducted before the Gracians moved their operation from France. Commander Thomas even met with the Prime Minister and the Chancellor of Nuclear Affairs before the ship even got to Germany. The fact that Germany was in the process of de-commissioning all of their Nuclear electrical generating plants meant that their DU stockpiles were in only two places.

The Uranium gathering amounted to over 94% of Germany's DU stockpile. This produced more fuel then the LRGEV167 required but the processing was allowed to continue to help Germany save on de-commissioning costs. They were thankful for this gesture and stated that the entire uranium processing effort carried out by the Gracians saved the country approximately € 85 million.

Centuries ago, the Gracians developed a cure for the dreaded Alzheimer's Disease. As a further token of their appreciation, Commander George presented the German Chancellor with an extensive medical journal that detailed a suggested path forward for an eventual cure. This journal was not a tutorial or instructional manual on how to develop a cure, because some of the procedures and pharmaceuticals have yet to be developed by the Earthlings, however it will act as a guide and possibly save them from going down certain research 'rabbit holes.'

Chapter 32

Departure

Their fuel problem solved, Commander George and the crew of LRGEV167 once again depart Earth and are currently in a staging location about 500 miles above the planet. It will take about one day to inspect, test, and prepare the craft for the long passage back to Planet Grace. It is a trip that the commander and crew are looking forward to.

After coordinating departure procedures with his officers, Commander George find himself with some 'quiet time'. He reflects upon his experiences on Earth. He thinks of the people he has met, from Ann Maloch, the NASA Director's secretary, the Director himself, the medical staff at the hospital, the heads of states and the technical people who helped with the fueling operation. All of these people were kind, helpful and willing to assist in any way to ensure a successful result whatever the task was. The camaraderie, spirit, and cooperation of the workers was gratifying. As he went about thanking the people who helped them, he heard expressions like, "No problem. This is how we roll." or "Glad we could help; this is how we get things done on earth." or "Happy to help someone in need" and similar rejoinders.

And yet at the time of his visit, there were wars being fought, crimes being committed, people being murdered, people starving, and still others in desperate need of rudimentary medical treatment. The paradoxical nature of life on Planet Earth was difficult and almost impossible for him to grasp. He saw it as a huge disconnect between different groups of Earth's citizenry. And sadly, the people who were aware of the difference, and there were many, treated it as unimportant or with indifference.

Commander George's thoughts were interrupted by a message from Space Command Headquarters requesting that he stand by for a conference call from several Directors of 'The Center'. He figured this must be important as he had never before heard of the Center calling a space explorer vehicle.

Chapter 33

Call From The Center

In about an hour, Commander George is contacted by the Center.

"Hello Commander George, this is Zon, Lead Director of the Center. With me is Operations Director, Firth and Financial Director, Sim. There are also 6 other directors present, making us a group of nine. We hope you trip is going well. We hear you actually made a landing on Earth to deliver the 3 astronauts you rescued from a runaway space station vessel. The rescue was very admirable, and we commend you for it. While on earth, we also hear you gathered some much needed fuel to help get you back to our planet. That was very resourceful of you Commander."

"Thank you sir."

Zon, "I will get right to the point. As you know, while your vehicle was in close proximity to Earth and actually on the planet itself for 22 days, the LRGEV167 crew had been sending back data about the operations of the Planet Earth. We have received information regarding governance, politics, social behavior, religions, the environment, conservation practices, and even recreational activities that take place on the planet. Based on this data and previous activities we have observed, our conclusion is that Earth is a hostile place that probably will not or cannot change its ways. Quite frankly, we are surprised that this planet continues to exist; that it has not destroyed itself.

We did not come to this conclusion lightly. We have known about Earth's existence for about 6,000 years. We have visited it 5 times in the last 3,700 years including your recent trip. We have found that civilization on Earth started as small nomadic groups, who for the most part, were peace loving people living in harmony with themselves and their surroundings. However, when one of their group started to lead or take charge it appears the power of leadership corrupted him, or her, and peace and harmony gave way to adversarial behavior towards, not only their own people, but outsiders as well. We saw Middle Easterners enslaving Middle Easterners; Africans capturing and selling Africans; Central and South Americans capturing and enslaving Central and South Americans; North Americans fighting each other for the purpose of stealing wives, children, and material possessions; and the oppressiveness of the Asian sub-continent "Caste" system. We have witnessed the outright brutality of leaders trying to force political ideologies on the very people they claim to want to help, all in the name of 'making things better'.

Over the course of our visits, we have observed changes but not improvement. And due to steady advances in weaponry development, we see destructive forces growing ever stronger and more brutal. We are of the opinion that eventually, Earth will destroy itself. But we have no idea when. And therein lies the problem.

Commander, you might ask yourself; Why do we even care if Earth destroys itself? After all, we are 26 light years away from that planet. Normally, that would be a good question. But we understand that certain countries on Earth are planning to place weaponized satellites in orbit above earth and to export weapons and to make defense colonies on their moon and worse, they probably will be nuclear. We view this exporting of weapons into space as the beginning of a threat to the overall peace and tranquility of the Milky Way and eventually a threat to our planet. Granted, this threat may not materialize for centuries, but we believe it will happen. The expansion of Earth's fighting regions is bound to continue and will not be reversed.

We do not want to 'wait and see what happens'. Our Threat Assessment System has advised that we should deal with this problem now. The Systems recommendation is to eradicate Earth. We will do this by hacking into the control systems of the 10 Earth countries that possess approximately 13,000 nuclear weapons and use these arsenals to destroy the planet. The actual hacking and firing of the necessary number of weapons needed to destroy Earth will originate from your vehicle, Commander. We will send you detailed instructions on how to go about the hacking and the subsequent firing of the weapons. It should not be a difficult task given the advanced computer systems aboard LRGEV167.

To anyone watching, if indeed there is anyone, it will appear as just another unexplained explosion in space.

"Do you have any questions, Commander?"

Commander George, "Yes, I do have some questions. First and foremost, we Gracians are a peaceful, tolerant, and loving race of people. So how is it that we can decide to annihilate billions of people, most of whom have no control over what their leaders say or do?"

Zon, "We agree that leadership is the cause of the planet's shortcomings. But we feel that if current leaders were eliminated, replacements would move up from the ranks and behave in the same, or perhaps in an even a more depraved manner. It has happened before on Earth. To really fix things - attitudes, mind sets, and philosophies - all must change, and we see no way of bringing that about. Leaders will never give up or alter their position of power. And if they did they would soon be ousted. The safety and protection of our planet comes first.

You said you had 'some questions' which means more than one. Please tell me what's next on your mind."

Commander George, "During some of Grace's past visits, including the most recent one, we have talked and even worked with the Earthlings. We have found them to possess many of the same qualities that we have. They may not be as intelligent as we are or enjoy our technological advantages, but they seem to be decent people who want to live their lives in an unobtrusive fashion. They have not contributed to this morass, and on the contrary, they have at times risen against it. Why then should they be eliminated?

Zon, "Granted they have risen up against, and even triumphed over the tyranny of some of their leaders, but these successes are usually temporary with the malicious people reconquering the good people. The Earthlings' own history proves this fact. This vicious cycle of good conquering evil and vice versa appears to be unending and has created countless wars and conflicts."

Commander George, "I do not believe it's that simple. There have been periods in their history of relative calm, and it could happen again. Why should we rob them of that chance to make things better for themselves?"

Zon, "What you say is true. But if you look at Earth's history over the past 5,000 years you will see more fighting and conflicts than peace and calm. And let us not forget the inhumane treatment of certain classes of people over this period of time. Taken as a whole, the people of earth have not behaved well towards each other. Even their early religious scriptures have one brother killing another.

Our Threat Assessment System shows that Earth will eventually develop the necessary technologies to explore the Milky Way Galaxy, and they will, in turn export their war-like traits and characteristics and horrible weapons to other habitable planets including Planet Grace and that is something we do not want. The Assessment further recommends that Earth should be eliminated, as soon as possible and that delaying this action will not change any of the threat predictions."

Commander George, "Sir, I still can't believe we have to take such strong action. Are there no other options available? Can we just try eliminating the evil leaders once again? How can we decide upon such a final and irreversible course of action?"

"Commander, I'd be surprised if you didn't ask these questions. As I mentioned, the care and safety of our planet and it's people are our number one priority. It trumps all other considerations. During our early history, on more than one occasion, we were attacked by forces beyond our galaxy. We survived these onslaughts and decided we needed to enhance our defense systems. Part of the defense build-up was to develop a threat assessment mechanism that would deal with any danger or threat to our well-being. The Threat Assessment System we developed does this by using thousands of historical data points, algorithms, and test scenarios. We have always followed the assessment's recommendations, and they have proven to be correct.

As far as simply removing the current installment of bad leaders, as I mentioned before, we feel that won't solve the problem.

Protecting our planet's well-being far outweighs any other consideration including time and collateral damage.

Commander, I hope that answers your question."

"It does."

"Now Commander, I have two questions for you. Can you carry out this mission? Do you have any problems with it?"

Commander George, "No sir I do not. I am honored that you took the time to discuss the situation with me. You have answered all my questions. And I am prepared to carry out my orders whenever my commanders tell me to do so."

Zon, "Thank you, Commander. We will need a little time to finalize plans. You will probably receive detailed orders in the next day or so.

When you return to Planet Grace, I would like to meet with you and hear about your entire mission."

Commander George, "Yes sir. LRGEV167 over and out"

The conversation with the center and the plan of action discussed were somewhat disconcerting to Commander George. On the one hand he is duty-bound to obey the orders of his superiors and with that he has no problem. He also believes that he and his crew can handle hacking into the nuclear weapon control systems and firing the weapons. If done properly the instantaneous firing of however many nuclear weapons it will take to do the job will be very humane to the Earthlings owing to the sheer force of the world-wide explosions. They will not know what hit them!

What is troubling him is seeing the faces of the people he has personally dealt with on the ground. These were good people, open and welcoming to him and his crew. They were working and living and doing their jobs. They were not fighting each other nor trying to force their wills on others. They were not part of the problem, not part of the evil. Why then, do they have to perish? Why do they have to be caught up in the 'solution'? Is there a better way than annihilating an entire planet?

Commander George goes about his day checking the ship and receiving reports about its space-worthiness. But also on his mind is his impending mission and more specifically the destruction of so many billions of people. After pondering the situation for most of the day and night he develops a possible alternative solution. The problem is he has no one to discuss it with. He cannot talk to anyone aboard the ship, and he does not know if anyone on planet Grace is aware of the plan other than the 9 center directors that participated in yesterday's video conference from the Center.

Nevertheless, he believes his idea may have a chance to be considered by the Center. But first he must find out how to reach them. They are the leaders of planet Grace, and one does not just pick up the phone and dial them any more than you would directly dial the President of the United States. His first call is to Grace's Mission Control where he asks to be connected to the Center.

"This is Phicon, director of Mission Control. Commander George, I see that your current location is within several hundred miles of planet earth. May I ask what your business is with the Center?"

"I was in contact with them yesterday and I want to follow up on that conversation."

"I do not see you having any contact with the Center yesterday."

"I was in contact with them, and it is most important that I talk to them again."

"Commander, I will have to get back to you on your request."

There is nothing Commander George can do but wait as his only point of contact with Grace, at this distance, is Mission Control. He returns to the job of getting the ship ready for the journey home. A short time later he receives a call from the Center.

"Commander George, This is Zon, Lead Director of the Center with me are directors Firth and Sim who were here yesterday. I apologize for the clandestine call but for security purposes, important communications like this, and the one yesterday are routed through a private back-channel network. As for Mission Control, we received your request and told them we would handle it internally. So, Commander, tell me, what is on your mind?"

"Well first of all let me say that I continue to be ready and willing to carry out the mission. And I agree with the overall assumptions issued by the Threat Assessment and the subsequent solution.'

"Thank you Commander."

"Also let me preface my comments by saying that, I along with several of my crew members, are the only living Gracians who have had actual recent contact with the Earthlings. Our reports on working with them are filled with positive comments. We found that they are very capable of getting things done but not always in the manner that we are used to seeing. There are many human characteristics that sometimes get in the way of their progress but in the end they get things done What concerns me is that we are not giving the Earthlings a reason for our concerns or a chance to correct them."

Zon, "We are of the opinion that the Earthlings are not capable of making the magnitude of change required to bring about global peace and harmony to their planet. Our Threat Assessment System bears that out. Any Earth group's attempting to do so would be perceived as weak or naive or even cowardly. They would not stand a chance of succeeding. The Earthlings history proves that. So why give them that opportunity?

Commander George, "We are harming so many because of so few. This hardly seem fair, so inhumane. This action is the antithesis of our fundamental belief system."

"Commander, yesterday you may recall talking about this. We both agree that Gracians are a fair and humane race of people. At the risk of being blunt, what could be more humane than almost instant annihilation? Especially if everyone perishes at the same time give or take a few moments. No one suffers. And remember they, as a group, have caused the problem. Our action is not punitive. We are not trying to punish anyone. We are simply addressing a problem that affects the peace and tranquility of our home."

"Commander, do you have any further comments on the plan?"

"No sir."

Zon, "Do you have any other comments regarding, perhaps an alternate way of handling this perceived threat? "

Commander George, "Actually, I do. Let me explain. There are 10 countries on Earth that possess Nuclear weapons. My plan would be to notify them and all of the other countries on Earth of our threat assessment and advise them of our concerns, specifically, the dangers of 'playing geopolitical chess' with Nuclear weapons. We will tell them that in order to make our point we will detonate one Nuclear weapon in each of the 10 countries. This will demonstrate to all citizens of Earth the actual destructive force of these horrible weapons.

We would then warn them that if, in say three years, they cannot make progress in abandoning their war-like ways and start living together in peace and harmony then we will return and destroy the entire planet."

Zon, "Do you have any other comments?"

"No sir, I do not."

Zon, "Commander your plan has merit. We at the center, like all Gracians, are fair and open minded. As such we will take your plan into consideration and reply to you by tomorrow. Does that satisfy you?"

Commander George, "Yes, it does and thank you for your consideration. LRGEV167 over and out."

Commander George is pleased that the call from the Center went well although he expected it might. After all, he was not challenging any authority he was simply offering his idea as to how things might be done differently. What surprised him was that they are willing to consider his plan.

The Center has always been open and approachable to the citizens of Planet Grace, and they have never acted in a dictatorial fashion. Their role has always been to guide and protect their planet based on the will of the people. They see Grace not as theirs to rule but a place to manage the affairs of its citizenry.

After a fitful night, Commander George awakens to find the good ship LRGEV167 fully prepared for service to travel home or to carry out the final orders from the center. His morning officers meeting is light and cheerful with the crew more than ready to travel on.

About midday the center calls.

"Commander George, This is Zon, with me again are directors Firth and Sim. We have reviewed your plan. And we have taken into consideration your insights based on actually visiting Planet Earth and interacting with some of it's residents. We have decided to adopt your plan. We made this decision based on the fact it will save many lives and it does give the Earthlings a reason to bring about much needed change and an opportunity to save their planet and themselves. Plus, it has a backup plan. If they are not able or willing to do what we are suggesting, three years is not a long time to wait. What say you to this decision Commander?"

"I appreciate the Center's considering and then following my suggestion. I will develop a detailed implementation package and send it off to you for approval. My crew will need instructions on how to 'hack' into the Earthling's various Nuclear control systems, and I will submit a list of the 10 targets to be destroyed. Once I receive the necessary approvals, we should be able to go ahead with implementation."

Zon, "OK Commander, we will see to it that you have everything that you need. Please give us updates as you move ahead with implementation. Is there anything else?"

Commander George, "Yes, given the sensitivity of this mission what about confidentiality? When can I talk to my crew about it? And also, Mission Control?"

Zon, "As far as your crew is concerned, I suggest you hold off discussing it until everything is approved and in place. However, if security starts to get in the way of your preparation, I suggest you talk to whoever you need to as it becomes necessary. It is your plan and your call. Someone from the Center will let you know when Mission Control has been notified. In the meantime, if they ask when you will be starting for home, tell them as soon as you receive final orders from the Center.

Is there anything else Commander?"

"That's all I have sir."

"Remember, you owe me a visit after you return home."

"Yes sir. LRGEV167 over and out."

Chapter 34

The Plan

The Plan of action has now been finalized. Commander George has a number of things to do among them:

1. Arrange for a meeting of world leaders, which is no simple task.
2. Develop a narrative explaining what will take place and why.
3. Select the 10 targets.
4. Hack into their respective nuclear weapon control sites.

By a stroke of good fortune, the United Nations General Assembly is holding its annual meeting in New York City in 9 Days. Most of the 193 member nations will participate live in person or by video conference. This technical innovation was installed to ease the logistical problems associated with getting all members to gather in New York City at the same time.

Commander George sees this as the perfect venue to advise world leaders of the Gracian's plan. He will use the video system, including its thirty foot screen which has been mounted in the main assembly hall. This will save him from having to make the 500 mile trip from his holding position in space to New York City and more importantly, eliminate the need for his personal security.

The commander knows that his initial appearance will be well received. However, the mood of the Assembly will change dramatically once his speech is delivered. After all he is going to criticize earth's behavior almost since its inception, tell them they are becoming a threat to the Milky Way Galaxy, tell them they must make enormous changes in their relationships with each other, and to make his point, tell them that he will be detonating a number of Nuclear weapons at varies locations on their planet. There will be questions, perhaps calls for his arrest and maybe even panic and violence. He is glad to be making this address from the safety of space and LRGEV167.

His problem will be getting on the agenda. He hopes the celebrity of his recent visits to Texas, France and Germany will help him with this.

After a number of failed attempts, he finally gets through to the U.N. Secretary General's office and makes his request to a staff member who is familiar with the 'Alien Visitor'. The staff member explains that this year's agenda is full and next year's is as well.

He then calls the German Chancellor and asks him to intercede. He tells the Chancellor that the message he has to deliver will have a worldwide effect on its citizenry and that the UN is the perfect place to deliver it. The Chancellor naturally asks what is the general nature of the address. Commander George explains that all will be revealed during the address, but he cannot disclose anything ahead of time. The Chancellor replies that this is most irregular. Commander George tells him that this is a very powerful and far reaching address that will affect all of mankind and its contents cannot be revealed beforehand. The Chancellor says he would like to help but he feels uncomfortable getting involved with such a vague and almost mysterious situation. He does, however, say that he is willing to call the Secretary General and urge him to listen to what the commander has to say.

The Secretary General knows who Commander George is and does agree to listen to what he has to say. A video conference is set up for 6:00 PM that same day. Commander Thomas delivers his comments and like the Chancellor, the Secretary's reaction is along the same lines. However, this time Commander Thomas tries some reasoning. He explains that he is an intelligent, reasonable person not given to flights of fancy or the bizarre and what he has to say is actually a warning that needs to be heard. He points out that he has come from afar to help with a mercy mission that saved three lives, and he has given advice to some of Earths scientist and researchers in order to help them with their discovery and development work. There is no reason to stop believing him now. The Secretary General asks how long it will take for his address and the commander tells him, 15 minutes. The Secretary thinks for a moment and then tells the Commander that he has his 15 minutes.

When news of the 'spaceship' commander's name was placed on the UN General Assembly's speaking agenda it caused quite a stir. Speculation regarding the subject matter of his speech ran rampant and the photos of the ship and its personnel appeared in the mainstream media together with all kinds of personal interest stories. But, to Commander George it simply means that step one is out of the way. He would work on step two, the speech, later. He goes on to step three, the targets.

There are 10 countries on Planet Earth that have nuclear weapons. According to Commander George', research, they can be divided into two groups. The first group he calls Defensive. They will not initiate the use of nuclear weapons. Their weapons are intended to deter other states from attacking with the promise of retaliation and possibly mutually assured destruction.

He calls the second group Offensive. They use their weapons as a nuclear deterrent as well as a threat to force their political agendas on others, or simply as a threat of usage against their perceived enemies. He believes this group would initiate usage of nuclear weapons. His classification follows.

Nuclear Weapons Classification

Defensive

China
France
India
Israel
Pakistan
United States
United Kingdom

Offensive

Russia
North Korea
Iran *

*Have not admitted to having nuclear weapons

Commander George admittedly, does not know much about the geography of Planet Earth. He has at his disposal maps and charts that show him many of its features from large urban areas to unpopulated wastelands and deserts. His plan is to release the ten Nuclear weapons in areas of their respective countries that have low to zero population thereby minimizing the human toll of destruction. He finds that eight of the ten countries have areas that fit this criteria. They are Russa, USA, China, Pakistan, India, Iran, Israel and North Korea. The two remaining countries, England and France have no such areas due to the number and layout of their towns, villages, and hamlets. No matter where the Nuclear weapons are detonated in these two countries, the loss of life will be significantly higher. This does not seem fair to Commander George, and it is his problem to solve.

The crew of LRGEV167 have received the 'hacking' instructions from their commander and have stealthily infiltrated the nuclear weapon control systems of the ten countries. They can assume firing control as soon as the order is given.

Chapter 35

The Speech

The speech writing, deciding how to handle England and France, and naming a nuclear detonation date are the only things to be completed. Commander George returns to his office to start writing. The opening day of the UN General Assembly meeting, and delivery of his speech are three days away and he is thankful that he will not be going to New York City to deliver it. He is 500 miles above Earth.

It has taken him two days of writing and rewriting, and the speech is now complete. He will now submit it to the Center for approval.

The day has arrived, and Commander George is 'on the air' and ready to start his address.

"Good Evening Ladies, Gentleman, and Diplomats to the United Nations. Thank you for allowing me to address this august body of world leaders. I am Commander Thomas George of Planet Grace's Long Range Galaxy Exploration Vehicle 167. I am speaking to you from outer space. Our current position is approximately 500 miles above the equatorial ring of your planet.

Planet Grace and Planet Earth have shared the Milky Way Galaxy since both of our planet's inceptions. Our Milky Way also includes Earth's 8 planet solar system, and other habitable planets, of which you may not be aware of, close to 300 moons, countless asteroids and comets and millions of stars, your Sun being one of them.

Plant Grace's explorers have discovered and visited 10 habitable planets which we found to be in various stages of their own evolution. Several had no human population, only animals, and vegetation and water. Others did have human populations. Common to all of the populated planets was the fact that they were living in peace and harmony with each other, and they had a goal of advancing themselves for the good of all of their inhabitants.

I am sorry to say that we did not see peace and harmony when we visited Planet Earth.

This is our fifth visit to Earth. The first was in the year 1299 BC during the Trojan War; a second time was in 623 BC during the Roman Conquest. We waited a good while, until 1864 AD, before our third visit only to witness the American Civil War. Our last visit was on March of 1943, when we witnessed the chaos of your World War II and the horrific, inhumane, treatment of millions of innocent men, women and children as directed by just 3 people, Adolf Hitler, Josef Stalin and Hirohito and their legions of misguided hellions. On each visit, including this past one of several weeks ago, we *observed a planet struggling with development, and civil unrest; of propagating slavery and maltreatment of certain 'lower classes' of its citizenry, and almost constant fighting somewhere on the planet for one cause or another.*

Not so long ago, a new form of weaponry, called 'nuclear bombs' had been developed. Earth has a combined arsenal of some 13,000 of these powerful weapons. They are held by 10 or so countries. The fact that these countries use them as deployment threats against each other and other countries simply astounds us. Have you no idea of this weaponry's destructive power? Especially if you fire them in 'salvos' at each other. You use them as if they were slings and arrows. They are not!

What disturbs us Gracians the most is that several of Earth's countries are planning to place weapons in Earth-orbiting 'Defense Satellites' and locations on the moon. If it does not happen initially, how long will it take before these weapons become nuclear? And as Earth continues to make technological advancements, how long will it take before these weapons are exported to other parts of our Milky Way along with all of earth's other, "warring habits."

We Gracians cannot and will not let this happen. For we see future expansion as a threat to our planet and our way of life. It will also pollute our beautiful Milky Way which, as far as we can see, does not have any of these undesirable earth-born weapons or characteristics.

We are, therefore, asking Earth to mend its ways. We are asking it's people and in particular their leaders, to stop the fighting for world domination, land grabs, and religious beliefs; to stop the maltreatment and enslavement of the poor, less fortunate populaces and to start treating your fellow man with respect, assistance, and kindness; to work together for the common good of all.

We ask that all nuclear weapons be destroyed and the total cessation of all future manufacturing of these terrible weapons.

In order to make our point about nuclear weapons and to remind all earthlings how destructive they can really be we will be detonating one in each of the countries that have these terrible weapons. They will come from each country's nuclear weapon arsenal. We have taken over control of each of your nuclear weapon firing systems and detonation will start shortly after the conclusion of my speech.

After that Earth will have three years to comply or to at least make significant progress in achieving a peaceful coexistence including the elimination of nuclear weapons. If we don't see progress being made, we will return and annihilate Earth thereby eliminating it as a threat to our planet and the Milky Way Galaxy.

I hope you heed this warning and comply with our requests. If you do not, the consequences will be dire.

The large video screen in the UN General Assembly Hall then goes blank.

Chapter 36

Reaction and Follow Through

A ttendees are not certain what to make of what they just heard. Most think it is an elaborate hoax and start to criticize the Secretary General for letting it air. But there are some in the assemblage that do believe the message. These people represent lesser countries and actually welcome the dictates. The assembly is now in disarray and the Secretary General calls for an adjournment of the session with a promise to follow up on the entire business.

Meanwhile world media has exploded. Speculation abounds and words like Armageddon, obliteration and eradication are being thrown about at will. Everyone from Joe the barber to retired diplomats and military generals are being interviewed for their opinions on what was said at the UN. Futures on the Stock Market are down 3,200 points. Next day school sessions have been cancelled, and the FAA is considering ordering a ground stop for all U.S. airports.

Soon after the speech, the Air Force base at Castle Rock, Colorado, reports that they are locked out of their nuclear Weapon Control Center system. Military bases in China, Russia and France also discover similar situations with their

Nuclear weapon control systems. But each country's military is not talking to one another for fear of discovery that their nuclear systems and offenses are not operating, and they will be perceived as vulnerable if word gets out. The irony is by not talking to each other they do not know just how widespread the problem really is.

About 2 hours later a large Hydrogen bomb detonation occurs In the Krasnoyarsk Arai area of Russia. This country was noted for their aggressive Nuclear weapon threats, so they were first on the detonation list. Two hours later a similar detonation occurs in the desert area of Pakistan. This time an Atomic bomb was used. Next a Hydrogen bomb was detonated in the high desert of Navada, USA. This was followed by another Hydrogen bomb detonation in China's Gobi Desert. Atomic bombs were than detonated in desert areas of India and east of Israel's Asfar settlement in the West Bank. Then a Hydrogen bomb was detonated at North Korea's main nuclear arsenal at Tonaghae. Due to their previous threats of Nuclear bomb aggression and depending upon their reaction to this detonation, a second and even a third detonation may be required to quell North Korea's desire to threaten the world with its Nuclear weapons even though they are locked out of their control system. Iran's Nuclear research and development center at Natanz, in the central desert received two Hydrogen bomb detonations followed in closer order of each other. This was done for two reasons. First like North Korea, Iran has demonstrated an extremely aggressive Nuclear threat posture when dealing with their perceived enemies and damage to their to Nuclear weapon facility is deemed necessary to halt any further Nuclear bomb production. Second, the facility is built 300 feet below ground and is difficult to inflict serious damage with conventional bombing.

Commander George has sent communiques to France and England advising them that they will be spared the Nuclear detonations because their compact geography. Nuclear bombs detonated in either of these two countries would cause extensive urban destruction and a disproportionate numbers of fatalities. He pointed out that the other countries had deserts or unpopulated areas in which to detonate the bombs and thereby minimize mortality rates. He also mentioned that France and England never demonstrated any nuclear aggression or threats, and they possessed Nuclear weapons purely for deterrent purposes.

Government reactions to the detonations were predictable. Russia blamed the United States working in concert with Ukraine. The United States held an emergency session with Congress, and two committees were formed to study the situation. China moved ships and a million soldiers to its borders to bolster protection, Iran blamed Israel and the United States for the detonations, Israel denied having nuclear weapons and North Korea threatened the world with annihilation, starting with South Korea and the United States.

Chapter 37

The U N Speech + 3 Years

It has been almost three years since Commander Bou delivered the Gracian Speech at the U N forum in New York City. At the time, there was significant acceptance of the speech's concepts by the world's population. They accepted the deadline and embraced the thought of world peace and all of the positives that came along with it. They were indeed pleased, albeit naively so, that positive change was being advanced. The six nuclear bomb detonations certainly brought home the seriousness of the matter and the Gracian's resolve to follow through.

The United Nations had taken the lead in developing a workable plan to affect the necessary changes laid out by the *Gracian Ultimatum*, as the General Assembly called it. They formed a worldwide committee and prepared and approved a list of major items that needed to be accomplished. The committee head a former chairman of the World Olympics committee and one of the few people on earth who had the global experience and organizational skills to direct a task of the magnitude and criticality the Ultimatum demanded.

Not all countries believed in the Ultimatum. Some doubted its authenticity and even its origin. Major players in this were known for their anti-Europe or anti-West positions. They claimed the Ultimatum to be some sort of deception concocted by the West in an attempt to bring about nuclear disarmament which in turn would weaken their defensive fighting capability. Some countries in the group were affected by the nuclear bomb detonations, but they looked upon them as also part of the West's nuclear disarmament plan.

This group paid no attention to the Ultimatum and simply went about their business as usual. There was hardly any mention of the Gracian decree in their domains.

The exuberance of the people in favor of the Ultimatum was short lived. Not too long after it was announced, this group began to notice that in spite of all the rhetoric, nothing was actually being done to prepare for compliance. Everyone agreed that action was needed but no one wanted to make the first move to start the process.

The people believed that state and nation governments should initiate the action, after all they are the first line of defense in protecting its citizenry. However, this was not the case. The governments offered little advice and no real action. When they did report something it was infrequent, uninspiring and totally lacking in direction. In time their responses melded into a unified theme of hope that the

Gracians meant Earthlings no real harm and that they would offer some type of reprieve option.

Action on a global was not happening. The U. N. special "Compliance Committee" seemed to generate a lot of thoughts and words but action was not taking place. Meetings between U. N. member states were arranged but all too often the no-shows outnumbered the attendees. Hesitation in initiating action, taking the lead, going out on a limb or worse, being abandoned by all those who promised to follow, seemed to deter any real movement. Everyone seemed to be waiting for the "other guy' to move first.

Even the U. N.'s Security Council could not bring about any action. This may be in part because of how the council is organized. The U.N. itself is made up of 194 of the 209 countries on Earth; 15 breakaway states have no formal U. N. recognition.

The Security Council is made up of 5 permanent and 10 non-permanent members. The 5 permanent members are the United States, United Kingdom, France, China, and the Soviet Union. Their attempt at taking action was hindered by the fact that two of the members do not believe that the Gracian threat is real and therefore they do not see the need to take any action. The 10 non-permanent members are elected by the U. N. General Assembly for 2 year terms. They are privy to certain global security briefings and other

Council business, but they have no voting power over any decision or actions taken by the 5 permanent members.

Religious groups make up the single largest group of people on Earth. But they too were ineffective in organizing any type of compliance movement. They made attempts at unity, they preached, and they prayed but nothing tangible came of it.

One group that had not lost sight of the reality or the consequences of non-compliance were the people involved in the actual rescue. NASA personal, emergency responders, hospital workers and the astronauts and their families all witnessed firsthand the Gracian's rescue and the medical skills that saved the astronauts lives and brought them safely back to Earth. They realized the Gracian's abilities were far superior to those found on Earth and, the Gracians were more than capable of carrying out the actions they claimed if the edict was not obeyed. People from this group often appeared on news and talk shows, in newspaper articles, and as guest speakers at technical seminars expounding the need for Ultimatum compliance and the possible consequences if they were not followed. But sadly, they could not get the most avid pro-Ultimatum groups to get motivated into acting.

As the clock ticks on towards the 3 year deadline, support for action continues to wan and skepticism grows among the Ultimatum's supporters. They have become less and less concerned even though the threat of annihilation is still present. It is like a feeling of indifference; a malaise has settled in, and they are just accepting whatever will happen.

The deadline imposed by the Gracian Ultimatum is now 7 weeks away. The Gracians have not been heard from since their initial address at the U.N. forum, and no one on Earth knows how to communicate with them.

Various military and Space Research groups have sent radio messages out into space hoping to contact the Gracians with the thought that they would perhaps communicate back to Earth. But none of these groups have received a reply. However, the Gracians have heard the Earth's communications and have chosen not to reply for concern of interrupting any progress Earth might be making to bring about the changes outlined in their Ultimatum. The Gracians plan has been to wait for the three year period to expire before they contact or perhaps even re-visit Earth.

In an effort to take some sort of action, the U.N. has recently polled their member nations and asked for their comments on the pending Gracian Ultimatum deadline. The vast majority has said that they have not been successful in taking any real action. Most also believe that they will be left alone and that no harm will come to them from the Gracians.

These responses from the member nations have prompted the U.N. to take the unusual step of issuing a communiqué to all citizens of Earth. This is what the U.N. had to say:

"To all Citizens of Earth. You are no doubt aware that approximately three years ago a representative from the Planet Grace addressed the United Nations General Assembly in New York City. In this address the representative laid down demands to all people of Earth that improvements must be made to our way of life in order to make our planet a better place in which to live. Further, the Gracian representative said that if changes were not made within three years, the Gracians would return and destroy our planet using weapons from our own nuclear arsenals.

Since the time of the address, we have not heard from the Gracians. We have tried to communicate with them, but our attempts have been met with silence. We strongly believe that the Gracians have abandoned their plans for Earth, and they have moved on to other galactic pursuits.

We therefor advise that you disregard the threats made by the Gracians and go on about your lives as normal.

Sincerely, The United Nations Secretary General

Other than making speeches, holding meetings, writing letters, and making attempts to communicate, perhaps there is nothing else to be done on a worldwide level. Perhaps organizing ny sort of global compliance for the Ultimatum's demands was just too formidable a task for the world's population and one that just could not be accomplished. Periodic reminders from the Gracians may have helped, but no communications were received.

Now, the deadline is less than 2 months away.

Chapter 38

Gracian Update

It has been 2 years and 10 months since the Gracian's address to the United Nations where they outlined their expectations for Earthlings to make their planet a better place in which to live. The Gracians did not plan to follow up or monitor compliance during the 3 year period. Rather, at the end of the period, the Gracians would simply check and see what progress had been made.

As fate would have it, one of planet Grace's Long Range Galaxy Explorer Vehicles (LRGEV) was returning home from an outer galaxy trip to harvest Augusite, a mineral that the Gracians use in the manufacture of ultra long range proton laser telescopes.

Zon, Lead Director of The Center, Grace's governing body, makes a direct call to the LRGEV Commander. He gives him a full account of the edict and requests that he make several observational passes of the planet to check on compliance.

After doing so, and performing some monitoring of selected communications, the LRGEV commander reports that nothing appears to have changed on the planet since the rescue of Earth's three astronauts.

The Lead Director cannot believe what is being reported. He orders the LRGEV to make more exacting observations and to monitor additional conversations and broadcasts, exercising care not to be detected.

The second report from the LRGEV is the same as the first. Wars are being fought, threats of additional wars are being made, exploitation of resources is actually on the rise, and mistreatment and abuses of marginalized people is continuing.

The Lead Director and the Center's executive directors react with surprise and disappointment about what is being reported.

Chapter 39

The Astronauts – Life After The Rescue

It took a while for the attention, and the pure excitement of the rescue to lessen but almost three years later the event has faded away to just another story woven into the fabric of Earth's history.

Life for the three astronauts has also returned to normal. U. S. Air Force Captain, Francis (Frank) Hammel has been promoted to Colonel. He has transferred from NASA back to the regular Air Force and commands their flight school division for heavy aircraft, (C-130's and C 5- Galaxie Star Lifters). Frank made the change because it afforded him greater opportunities to fly airplanes, which is his first love, after his wife and children.

Frank is very happy with his Air Force career and thanks God for having a wonderful family. He realizes how fortunate he was to be rescued by the Gracians and how lucky he is to be alive.

The Gracian Ultimatum very much concerns him. Having been in direct contact with the Gracians he knows that they are more than capable of following through with their edict. The lack of government action disappoints him very much. From the start of the ultimatum three years ago, there has been very little action on the government's part. They simply offered empty rhetoric but no real definitive action. What are they waiting for? Do they think they can wait this out and it will simply go away? Isn't our government supposed to protect us? We may very well be talking about imminent peril. This is potentially a grave situation and yet we are hearing very little from our leaders. Frank is very frustrated that personally, he cannot do much about it.

In spite of these concerns, he has managed to put the Gracian situation on the back burner. After all, he has a family to protect and care for, a job to perform, and these are the most important things in his life. In regard to the ultimatum, he does feel that as time expires, the Gracians will offer some type of reprieve with, of course, some very tough conditions attached. He can only hope and pray that this will come to fruition.

The second astronaut, Gloria Fan is still with NASA. She is continuing her work in the biological area of space exploration and is still the Co-chair of NASA's agricultural research team. Gloria has recently accepted a professorship at the University of California, Davis and she now splits her time between the college and the NASA Research Center in Houston TX.

Gloria was on her third trip to the ISS when she was rescued by the Gracians. She is saddened that ISS no longer exists having been destroyed by the meteor shower, but she lightheartedly thinks that maybe she will be doing some of her future biological work on the Moon or perhaps Mars.

Between her NASA work and her professorship duties Gloria has a very active life. She rarely thinks of the rescue. But she does often think of the Gracians and their ultimatum. Like Colonel Hammel she is concerned about the lack of action by anyone on earth especially given the threats of the ultimatum. She has discussed this on several occasions with the Colonel and like him believes that the Gracians will intervene at the last minute. She feels she has to maintain this feeling of hope to keep herself from falling into despair about the situation. This ultimatum does affect her, particularly when thinking about the future. The Gracians have to come through for her. She just wants the deadline to pass, one way or the other, so she can continue with her life if she has one.

The third crew member to be rescued from ISS by the Gracians was Dr. Rakib Rajbir a brilliant aerospace engineer who works for NASA. Ironically, he was on board the ISS to study the feasibility of extending the stations service life beyond its current 30 year term which expires in 2030. Needless to say, with the destruction of the station, his work came to an abrupt end.

Rakib, who is married with two children, continues to work with NASA in Houston, Texas. He currently heads up a group of NASA engineers and technicians who interact with Contractors such as GE Aerospace and Space X. Although currently working at NASA Houston, Rakib has not given up on his dream of flying to the Moon or perhaps even Mars.

Rakib is also a part of a Top Secret group of NASA officials who are working on a confidential project involving the Soviet Union. As mentioned previously, several countries in the world feel that the ISS was deliberately destroyed as part of an elaborate hoax perpetrated by the United States to foster worldwide nuclear arms elimination. Russia is one of those countries.

The Russians claim that ISS was not destroyed by a meteor but rather it was blown up by the three American astronauts occupying the station shortly after the two Russian cosmonauts left for home. The cosmonauts' departure was just weeks before the station was destroyed. The Russians claim that they have debris from the resulting mishap that was not destroyed as station fell to Earth. They claim this debris clearly shows evidence of explosions. The Russians have not shared any of this information, or the debris material, with anyone outside the Soviet Union.

The Russians say it is their intention not to disclose their discovery to any other countries if the United States is willing to compensate them for the loss of their space station assets.

They put the reimbursement amount at 900 billion Rubles or just over 10 billion U.S. Dollars. The Russians did have a sizable stake in the ISS. They built and launched the first module, named Zarya, into orbit. Since then, the Soviets had built and launched a number of additional modules, and supplied the ISS with shuttle service, materials and cosmonauts up until the time the station was destroyed.

In further support of their claim, the Russians **referenced a recent quote by a high U.S. official that the ISS had become obsolete and should be "de-orbited" and destroyed.**

The United States has dismissed this claim as sheer folly. However, they are giving it their attention, and they are investigating what the Russians are saying. This is proving to be somewhat difficult given the current strain of diplomatic relations between the two countries. Plus, the White House does not want this story to be headlined around the world no matter how ridiculous it may be. They feel that given the state of American and worldwide news reporting, the White House sees how this story could be spun into a believable falsehood.

Rakib, being a technical person sees just how ridiculous the Russian's claim is. The sheer logistics of putting together what they claim would alone prohibit it from being implemented.

He is also not concerned about the threats contained in the Gracian ultimatum. He feels that the lack of follow up communication by them indicates that the Gracians never had any intention of harming Earth's populace and have moved on from this whole business.

Chapter 40

What Earthlings Are Thinking

E. Theodor Nelson is the Chairman and CEO of a major Scandinavian automobile manufacturing company. He is also a member of the World Economic Council and is this year's Chairman of the World Economic Forum. Like many of his fellow industrial leaders, he keeps his opinions private including what he thinks about the Gracian Ultimatum.

In the case of this ultimatum, Mr. Nelson believes that whatever was going to happen would happen and there was nothing that anyone on Earth could do about it. This belief is rooted in an **Old Norse philosophy which is strongly fatalistic.** It basically says, "that no man can ultimately escape his fate". This belief applies to all classes of society, from kings to paupers. This fatalism encourages a man to live a life of courage and fortitude. This spirit is famously embodied in Nordic literature which emphasizes that the only lasting thing in the world is the noble name one gains by living a life filled with noble deeds. Like most Scandinavians, Mr. Nelson cares a great deal about his fellow man and is very understanding and tolerant of their ways regardless of their background, ethnicity, or culture.

Mr. Nelson is not overly concerned about what the Gracians are calling for in their edict. He believes that the world would be a far better place if their demands were implemented but he also realizes that it will probably not happen. When the Gracians do find out about the Earth's non-compliance, and they soon will, he thinks that rather than punish the people of earth by destroying the planet, they will dictate a new edict that will deal with what they perceive as our malevolent ways.

++++++++++

Richard Ravenu is a fourth generation banana plantation supervisor who lives and works on the West Indian island of St Lucia located in the Lesser Antilles. St. Lucia is 238 square miles in land area with a population of 190,000 people. It was initially inhabited by the Arawak and Carib Indians until it was discovered by Christopher Columbus during his third voyage to the new world in1498-99. About 20 years after Columbus, and for the next 4 centuries, colonization took place by the Dutch, French and finally the British. During this period, agricultural farming and export was developed, and slavery was introduced. In 1979 St. Lucia gained its independence from Great Britian.

Geographically, St Lucia is a scenic and picturesque island with mountains, hills and valleys covered with lush tropical foliage. White sandy beaches, and a large rain forest also complement the island's ecology. But this Eden-Esque setting is marred by poverty and high unemployment.

Richard Ravenu realizes his good fortune of being employed by one of St. Lucia's 600 banana plantations. He makes a decent living by St. Lucia standards and is comfortable with his life. His world evolves around his work, supporting his family of 7 children by 5 different woman and an occasional trip to Vieux Fort, to watch the cock fights and to play dominoes with his fellow St. Lucians.

Although Isolated from most of the world, Richard is aware of global events thanks to the British Broadcasting Corporation's (BBC) news service. He listens to the 6:00 PM World News Broadcast every evening on his 60 year old Grundig Majestic Type 97 Lamp Radio. He has been following the Gracian Edict story almost since it began. He is not concerned, nor does he feel threatened by it.

In the first place Richard believes that the Gracian's will not harm him or his fellow St. Lucians. Good or bad they are not responsible for the current state of the world. In his simple straight forward thinking, Richard sees St. Lucians as growing bananas, fishing and providing nice places for North American and European tourists to visit, particularly in the winter months. No! The Gracians may want to punish the people who made the current world the hostile place but that does not include the St. Lucians. They will leave us alone. "Doux pour des jours!" *("Sweet for days!", a French Antillean Patwa saying)*

++++++++++

Shana Carmichael was born and raised in East Orange, New Jersey, a bustling suburb of New York City. She was one of three children born to her mother, Sharleen, a practical nurse in nearby Newark City Hospital and her dad, Hampton who drives for a local commuter bus line. By most accounts Shana has had a normal childhood. Her parents owned their own home, which spared her the difficulties of living in crowded public housing. They sent all three of their children to parochial school and they all went on to graduate from college. Shana was the oldest child, so she enjoyed the privilege of having her own room which she relished and closely guarded from the prying eyes her two younger siblings. Her travels through her adolescent years consisted of family trips to the Pocono Mountains, upstate New York, and lots of bus trips (her dad had free passes) to places in New York City. Her dad, Hampton enjoyed being on the water therefore, some of these trips included Circle Line Tour Boat trips around Manhattan, to the Statue of Liberty, and to Bear Mountain.

Shana graduated from Montclair State with a teaching degree and got a job teaching biology at a local high school.

It was there that she meet her future husband Harrison DuFore. The couple now have two children.

Shana has followed the Gracian edict very closely ever since it was announced at the U.N. forum. She immediately understood the ramifications of non-compliance. She and Harrison have had a number discussions between themselves, their clergyman, and their parents but it is still an open ended issue. No one seems to have an answer, not the government, the church, nor their family. Shana sees it as a black cloud hanging over everyone. And she is especially concerned about the affect it will have on her children.

++++++++++

Yoshira Ogawa is a pilot, recently retired from Japan Air Lines (JAL) after 43 years of service. Before retiring, the last plane he captained was a Boeing 787 Dreamliner. Aviation was Yoshira's life. It was also in his family history. His father trained to be a Kamikaze pilot during the latter stages of WW II only to be denied action due to a shortage of planes to fly. The Ogawa family has lived in Japan for many generations, but they do have a vague ancestral connection to the HAN people of China.

The country of Japan has a long and storied history from the rise and fall of emperors, to rule by samurai warriors, to isolation from the outside world, and to expansion over most of Asia, which was followed by defeat, and rebirth.

Japan is predominantly a secular society where people prioritize harmonious relationships and the fulfillment of social duties over personal individuality. The values of order, harmony, and self-development are fundamentals and anchor Japanese social interactions. Similarly, religious practices underscore the significance of maintaining harmonious relations with both humans and spiritual entities and adherence to social obligations within the family and community frameworks. In Japanese mythology, deities demonstrate both love and anger.

Mr. Ogawa is very much concerned by the threats contained in the Gracian Ultimatum, and more importantly the complete lack of action by the people of the world. He believes that at least some type of "Good Faith" effort should be put forth by a group, or state, or country to show some compliance. He believes that the Gracians will take some sort of action, or worse, they will completely follow through with that they say.

The people of Japan, including Mr. Ogawa know first-hand what the detonation of a nuclear weapon can due, especially to a densely populated area. The memorials at Hiroshima and Nagasaki stand as stark reminders of the horrors, devastation and the cost of human life that just one of these bombs can inflict.

His concerns are amplified by the fact that today's nuclear bombs are much larger and more powerful, and the Gracians are talking about using many of them. Mr. Ogawa truly believes that their action will cause the end of the world and it's civilization and he is powerless to do anything about.

Since the U.N. address Mr. Ogawa has become completely indifferent. He now lacks feelings, emotion, interest, or concern about the future. He is suppressing emotions, excitement, motivation, and even passion. He is living in an apathetic state waiting for the bombs to drop.

++++++++++

Orville Williams was born and raised on a sheep ranch in the Wind River basin of Wyoming. The farm was in his family for three generations and it was currently owned by his parents Marge and Hardwick Williams. As well as sheep, the Williams also keep hogs, chickens, some beef cattle and horses to work the ranch.

In high school, Orville was a standout quarterback for the local football team. Shortly after high school he volunteered for the US Army. After Basic Training, Orville was selected and qualified to become a Green Beret. After completing that training, he shipped out to Iraq and Afghanistan where he would spend three tours of duty over the next four years.

At first Orville was a gung ho soldier. He loved fighting for his country and helping to protect and support his brothers in arms. But somewhere during his final tour of duty, in Afghanistan, he became disillusioned with the war and in particular the politics that were driving it. He had several assignments as a liaison officer between local village warlords and the U. S. military. Here he got to know the Afghan people, and their culture and their way of life. He learned that they too did not want war, nor did that want any foreign military occupation or outsiders telling them to run their country. They simply wanted to be left alone to continue their way of life as it had been for centuries before conflict and terrorism raised its ugly head and the religious zealots took over. Orville did not agree with all of the Afghani principles and philosophies. For example, how they treated their woman and their strict adherence to Shair law. But this was Afghanistan, and not the United States and there were not many comparisons between the two.

Orville began to question the purpose of the conflict. He understood the United States' aim to eliminate terrorists and win over Afghan people, but this goal became increasingly unclear. Despite his doubts, Orville remained committed to the Army and fought on. Given the uncertainty of victory and the complexities of the combatants, he believed it was still worthwhile continuing until the end of his tour. Upon returning home, he chose not to re-enlist, deciding that he no longer wanted to be part of the army and the fighting.

A short time after settling back into life in Wyoming, Orville also realized ranching was not something he wanted to do for the rest of his life. Actually, he did not know what he wanted to do. In order to help clear his head and figure things out, he decided to take some time off, tour the Western United States, see the sights, visit the national parks and hopefully get some clarity and direction for his life.

His grandfather had a 14 year old Hemi-Head Chrysler 4 door which he lent to Orville for his trek. Orville then, by coincidence, reunited with his high school sweetheart at a church social and after some brief time together, they were off on their grand adventure. The two of them saw wonderful sights, mountains, prairies canyons and all the beautiful scenery the America West had to offer. There were lots of wild animals; they learned how to cook foil wrapped hamburgers, hot dogs, and baked potatoes on the Hemi's exhaust manifold while they were motoring along. They even developed a recipe for what they called a "400 Mile Roast".

The trip worked. After some time, they found themselves in the Texas hill country where they settled, got married, and went on to college. Charlene became a registered nurse and Orville became a CPA. He opened up a business in Arkansas. He and his wife had two children, a boy named Elmer, and a girl named Patricia.

Orville continues to carry some of the scars of war with him, and one was the fear that war would eventually come to the

United States. In order to protect his family against this possibility, he purchased a missile silo that was being decommissioned by the U.S. Air Force. He then had it converted it to a fallout shelter complete with life support systems, utilities, furnishings, and enough food for 3 years.

Several years ago, when Orville first heard of the Gracian's edict he was not concerned. He was prepared. "Let them come, bomb what they want, my family and I are ready, and we will be safe!"

++++++++++

Numerous reactions have been recorded around the world. Some are similar to those listed above while others have much stronger statements involving hate, blame, and anger.

Some actions have been talked about as well. The two most popular are one, we should arm ourselves to the teeth and attack the Gracians as soon as the show up. The other involves mass suicides just ahead of the bombings. This is a very popular option in Russia, Greenland, South Korea, Guyana, Suriname, and Uruguay.

Chapter 41

The Gracians Plan of Action

Zon is the current lead Director of the Gracian's 400 member governing body known as The Center.

Based on recent observations reported by one of Grace's LRGEVs that had recently passed by Earth, Director Zon sees that not only have the Earthlings not made any progress towards mending their errant ways, but it also appears that conditions have actually gotten worse on planet Earth. He sees no point in waiting any longer for Earth to act on the terms of the Gracian Ultimatum and has called a meeting of 14 higher echelon members of the Center's organization. He has also asked Akar Bou, Commander the LRGEV that actually carried out the astronaut rescue from the destroyed space station to attend. Commander Bou, known as Thomas George to the Earthlings, also gave the Planet Grace Ultimatum address at the U.N. General Assembly three years ago. Recently, Director Zon had put Commander Bou in charge of developing a plan to deal with Earth's non-compliance of the Gracian edict.

Director Zon opens the meeting:

"Greetings fellow Directors and Commander Bou. I have asked you here today to discuss the current situation on planet Earth. Following the astronaut rescue of three years ago, we made some observations which led us to believe that Earth was a very contentious place. I will not get into details because we have been over them before.

Based on what we observed following the rescue, our group considered a decision to completely destroy Earth in order to stop the possible spread of their malevolence to other planets in our Galaxy. We know of at least six other inhabited planets plus our own that could be affected

Shortly after the rescue, when Commander Bou was still on station above Earth awaiting clearance to return home, and upon hearing of our plan, he intervened using the argument that, "why would we eliminate the entire population of Earth due to the action of some of its leaders and power brokers"? He also reminded us of our own tolerance and benevolence towards other people.

Commander Bou argument was persuasive, and we decided to follow his advice. We had him address the leaders of Earth, at a U. N. General Assembly forum to explain our concerns regarding their misbehavior towards each other, their malevolence and the effect this would eventually have if it spilled out to the rest of the planets in our shared galaxy. We laid down actions that they must take to make their planet a kinder, more benevolent place, one with less conflict and a greater tolerance for each other. And we gave them three years to accomplish this task. Adding that if they did not comply with our edict in the given time frame, we would return and destroy Earth using nuclear weapons from their very own stockpiles. To make our point, we detonated five of these terrible weapons at various locations throughout their planet.

Recently we have made some close observations of Earth. We have found that in the past three years nothing has changed and actually, conditions have gotten worse. Personally, after giving the Earthlings a demonstration of our ability to activate and fire five of their nuclear weapons, I am astounded that they have not taken any action to ward off the complete destruction of their planet.

Today we are here to discuss our options for the Earth situation, including the possibility of complete annihilation. Their own inaction has forced us to consider taking this drastic step. I have tasked Commander Bou with the development of a plan to carry this out. The commander was the ideal Gracian to handle this because of his previous experience in dealing with the Earthlings. As I mentioned, the Commander had previously advocated for leniency in dealing with them and he helped develop the Gracian Ultimatum. Now, I have asked him to evaluate the current Earth situation and develop a current course of action. I would like to hear what he has to say.

But before you speak, Commander, I would like to once again thank you for a job well done in connection with the space station rescue. This incident is a stark reminder of the perils that await each space explorer as he or she journeys into the Great Beyond, Commander Bou."

"Thank you Director Zon for your very complimentary words, and greetings to you Directors.

"I would like to address the most severe option first. The task of annihilating Earth is not a difficult one. Our technicians already know how to hack into Earth's nuclear weapon control systems as evidenced by the nine detonations we created three years ago. In our plan, the sequence of firings will be important because we have to be careful not to destroy the weapon control stations before we fire off the weapons they control. This will require some planning."

Director Ferth, Operations Director, "Do you have a count of how many nuclear weapons you may need? Does planet Earth have enough?

Commander Bou, "We estimate that we will need about 3,000 Nuclear weapons. There are an estimated 12,000 of these weapons in the combined arsenals of the 10 Earth nations that have these weapons. 3,800 are deployed; 5,700 are reserved, that is to say in storage, and not immediately ready for deployment; another 2,500 have been retired and awaiting dismantlement. These numbers are not exact. The weapon count could be as high as 13,000, however, most nuclear countries do not disclose much about their nuclear weapon arsenals.

It is interesting to note that on Earth up through the 1960's there were many more nuclear weapons held by the only two countries that possessed them, the United States and the Soviet Union. The exact number of weapons was never disclosed. Some say the figure was as high as 20,000!

Shortly after this period, these two countries started negotiating treaties that were supposed to limit the number of nuclear weapons each of them had. The treaties were known as the Strategic Arms Limitation Treaties or SALT I and II. After 8 years of negotiating, the SALT II agreement was signed but it was never ratified by the United States' Congress."

Director Zon, "Eight years to agree on the number of weapons each party would possess. No wonder the Earthlings could not comply with our edict in three years!"

Director Sim, Finance Director, "Are there different types of nuclear weapons?"

Commander Bou, "Yes, there are two main types, Atomic and Hydrogen, *Bombs*, as they are called by the Earthlings. Hydrogen bombs are usually more powerful. Within this group there is a class known as thermonuclear bombs. These weapons are designed to maximize the spread of lethal radiation while minimizing blast effects. Their primary

225

function is to harm human beings. Finally, there is also a weapon called a dirty bomb. It is not actually a nuclear bomb, and it is smaller and much less powerful. It is used to disburse radioactive material using conventional explosives. Its primary purpose is also to maximize harm to people. There are other "prototype" bombs in development. It seems the Earthlings are forever trying to improve these weapons and make them more powerful, deadly and destructive.

Director Zon, "We have none of these weapons, nor do we need them. I can only imagine how much time, money, and resources went into developing and manufacturing this many bombs. It certainly justifies our decision to annihilate Earth. I can just see the Earthlings exporting these weapons to their Moon and for that matter, to other habitable planets once they develop the inter-planetary delivery capability. Also, I suspect these planets will be just another thing for them to fight over."

Director Sim Finance Director, "How will you activate these weapons or bombs?"

Commander Bou," We will activate them "locally", that is from a LRGEV stationed about 500 miles above Earth. As mentioned, this approach was successful when we detonated the nine "demonstration" bombs three years ago.

Director Sim Finance Director, "Will you need more than one LRGEV?

Commander Bou, "Yes, we will need two. One will be the primary operating vehicle, and the other will act as a backup.

Director Zon, "When will you be ready?"

Commander Bou, "We could be ready to depart planet Grace in nine days' time. It will take seven days to travel to Earth, two full days to set up for bomb deployment and one or two days for actual bombings. So, the entire mission including our return home will take less than thirty days from our initial departure from Grace.

Director Ferth, Operations Director, "How affective will the annihilation be in terms of mortality? Will everyone die or will some Earthlings survive?"

Commander Bou, "Death will come very swiftly to most of Earth's population. We estimate that 99.99%, equal to 8.0 billion people, will perish during the initial bombings. The remaining .01% or approximately 800,000 will survive in various states of health from normal physical condition to critically injured. These people will survive because they will be either working underground or living in very remote places, not in close proximity to the bombing areas. How they will survive and for how long will be anyone's guess, but I suspect that most if not all will eventually succumb to injuries and illnesses caused by direct or indirect exposure to radiation.

In addition, most homes, buildings, factories and other structures will be destroyed or rendered unusable. Forests will be consumed by fire laid bare and most farmland will be destroyed. Huge volumes of water will be vaporized into the atmosphere and will than rain down planetwide creating tremendous flooding."

Director Ferth, Operations Director, "I must say that destroying a planet is not as easy as it sounds!"

Director Zon, "Do you have any other options to consider Commander? In your study of the Earth situation have you gained any further insights into their behavior?"

Commander Bou, "Yes, Earth's behavioral characteristics have puzzled us since we started our close-up review of their planet. We questioned how living under such oppressive conditions they could make such advancements in their civilization. We just don't know the answer to that.

 The answer to their malevolent behavioral question may be traced back to the Earthlings beginnings. Let me explain by reviewing a small page out of their ancestral history.

Currently, on Earth there are three very remote areas which have by and large escaped the reach of Earth's explorers. They are located in remote parts of the central sub-Sahara desert, the deep interior of the Amazon rain forest and the remote, swamp filled areas of central Papua New Guinea. Christian missionaries have visited these areas, and one, a

German missionary and his family of five, has even lived in Papua New Guinea with a native Fayu family for thirty years.

The Fayu are considered atavistic and have existed and remain untouched by any of earth's other societies since their Stone Age beginning. They inhabit New Guinea's swamp filled basin, are nomadic, live in small family groups, and are known primarily through fearful reports from their neighbors.

The Fayu have no government, leadership, or communal structure; they worship no higher power, God, or religion. The number one thing that has stymied Fayu population growth has been murder, that is to say Fayu killing Fayu. The reasons for the killings are bizarre even by Earth's standards and range from revenge for a prior killing of a family member to wanting to covet another's wife. There appears to be no punishment for murder in Fayu society, it is just a part of their way of life. Missionaries have recently made progress in curbing violence and killings within some of the Fayu bands, but this change is happening very slowly and may never completely come about. Actually, some missionaries have even lost their lives ministering to the Fayu and there are still some Fayu bands that remain uncontacted. To the Fayu violence and killing each other is not a bad or a good thing, it is just something that they do, and it has been a part of their culture, a part of their DNA since their beginning long ago.

So, my question is: Do other more advanced groups of Earth's societies have this same murderous characteristic or trait in their DNA as well? If so, it may explain the reason for their malevolence. After my review, I now believe that Earthlings are not capable of changing their ways and their relationships with each other because quite simply they are who they are.

We Gracians may have difficulty understanding this because it is the exact opposite of who we are and how we behave. Gracian leaders respect and care for the people they govern. They listen to what we Gracians have to say and earnestly try to do what's best for us. The Gracian people respect and support each other. The concepts of war, abuse, killings and violence are completely lost on the us. These thing just do not occur on our planet. We do have questions about our beginnings, but we know that we have behaved like this from as far back as our history can be traced.

I do have two other option worth mentioning. As I said previously, I still contend that many more innocent people will die in the annihilation than those who are maintaining Earth's current bad state of affairs, but this is a circumstance that will not change, and the threat of Earth's malevolent spread still remains. I believe that this spread threat is quite a long way off and we do have the option of waiting for a while longer, say fifty or a hundred years before any negative things emanate from Earth. And even if the timetable did accelerate, we have the capability of acting quickly to mitigate any of Earth's negative action should they occur.

A third option is a "surgical strike" operation. This would involve developing a list of Earth's leaders and their support staffs who are responsible for the current state of malevolence on their planet. This would include dictators, gangsters, terrorist, drug cartel heads and so on. These people would then be eliminated by highly trained specialist from our planet. If we are concerned about of any loss of Gracian life we could train members of our robot force to do the work. This option would take some time to carry out and would of course require Gracian boots on the ground, which may make it unacceptable, but it did come up in our planning and development sessions and I wanted to mention it.

So, to answer your question directly Director Zon, I see us as having three options to consider. One is complete annihilation, two take a wait and see approach and three use a Gracian "surgical" strike force to eliminate the "bad actors" on Planet Earth"

Director Zon, "Thank you Commander. Does anyone else have any final questions?

A collective "No" was heard.

Director Zon, "Commander Bou, I want to make sure I understand your position and I want to make certain that everyone in this room is fully aware of our options.

So, to summarize, three years ago, when we first brought up the Earth annihilation issue you successfully persuaded us to reconsider our action. Your argument was that we Gracians are a benevolent, caring, and tolerant people and we should not be considering annihilating anyone, let alone an entire civilization. We mentioned Earth's malevolent ways and how that could spread to other habitable plantes in our Milky Way, and you countered with the statement, "killing so many people when so few are actually responsible for Earth's current condition seems harsh to say the least".

Since then and based on your research and how you feel now, do you believe that annihilation is a viable option."

Commander Bou, "Yes, because I believe that Earthlings are not capable of making the needed changes."

Director Zon. "You also feel that taking a wait and see approach has merit because any spread threat is a long way off and we can always act to mitigate if need be. Is that correct?"

Commander Bou, "Yes that is correct."

Director Zon, "Commander Bou, do you have anything further to add?"

"No sir, I do not."

Director Zon, "Thank you, Commander. We appreciate the work you and you team have done to develop these options, and for you thoughts and comments regarding them. What you have offered gives balance to both sides of the issue.

I have one, actually two, final questions for you. How do you feel about carrying out this mission and do you have any personal issues with it?

Commander Bou, "No, Sir, I do not. I understand our decision-making process and I appreciate that you asked for my input. I believe the issue was thoroughly and properly discussed including our options. I will fully support any decision made on this issue and I am prepared to carry out whatever orders my commander gives to me.

"Does anyone one else have any further comments?"

"No. Thank you all for your input and your work over the past three years."

"Commander Bou raises a good point about acting now or perhaps waiting decades or even a century before acting on the Earth situation.

To that I say, there is no evidence that would even hint of any favorable change taking place on Earth over the next 10 or even 100 years. As a matter of fact, their recent behavior suggests that things are only getting worse. Also, the Earth situation came up on our watch and it is our problem to solve. It should not be left for future Center leaders to deal with. As for the third option, putting Gracian humans or robots on Planet Earth to carry out assassinations is just not something we want to do.

What say you Center Members? Should we act to annihilate or to wait and see? Or is there a need for further discussion?"

At this point, and after some quite discussions between the 14 directors, all agree that the option of annihilation should be followed.

Director Zon, "Then it is decided. I will convene a full meeting of all center members to review the issue and then schedule a planet wide vote on the proposed Earth annihilation action.

This meeting is adjourned."

Several days later a meeting of all 400 Center directors was held and after review and discussion on the Earth action an almost unanimous vote was cast in favor of annihilation. A general vote for all citizens of Grace was then held. The vote *for* annihilation of planet Earth was passed by a large majority of the Gracian population.

The clock on Commander Bou's annihilation plan had now started ticking.

Chapter 42

The Clock Is Ticking

It is less than two weeks before the compliance due date of the Grace Ultimatum. Commander Bou and his counterpart Commander Philo are preparing their LRGEV's for the mission to Earth. Crews will be briefed today. Any crew member who has an objection to the mission, be it moral, ethical, or political, will be excused and replacements will be arranged to fill any vacancies. This option is in keeping with one of Planet Grace's principles, which is that no Gracian, either civilian or military, will be asked to do anything against his or her will.

Each of the LRGEVs will carry a crew of 19 officers, 10 cadets, 18 navigational and engineering personnel, and 22 robots. After the crew briefing, it was noted that there were no opt outs from the mission.

No media coverage, sendoff celebrations, or fanfare of any kind were planned for the launch. Most Gracians simply viewed this mission as a defensive task that had to be performed for the greater good of the Milky Way Galaxy and in particular to protect its habitable planets.

The were a few Gracians who opposed the mission. These dissenters did not object to the annihilation action itself, but rather that the Gracian government should have given more consideration to the wait and see approach. Their reasoning was that the spread threat was not even close to happening and that Earth will have to develop a myriad of technical accomplishments and advances before it does. These dissenters represented a small minority of Gracians. They were pleased that their opposing views were heard and duly noted even though their suggested action was not followed. At least they had a chance to be heard.

Chapter 43

The Media Wakes Up

The Grace Ultimatum due date was a little over a month away. Earth was experiencing a slow news period. In order to fill the slump in news stories, one news outlet decided to do a "back page" story about the Gracian Ultimatum and its approaching due date.

At the time of the rescue, reporting of facts and events were clear, concise, and properly reported. Most information was easily available for research and fact checking.

However, this new article ignored the facts and went on to distort and even fabricate new details for the story. This was an obvious attempt to sensationalize the reading. For example, the article reported unfounded rumors about how the space station really "crashed", or how the three astronauts wound up "millions of miles from earth" and a report, allegedly suppressed by the United States government, that the alien rescue craft was crewed by hundreds of "extra-terrestrials with big heads and very large eyes" who apparently did not wear any clothing. But by far the most creative distortion was that the United States may have allegedly blew up the ISS because it was approaching the end its useful life and the government did not want to put any more money into the ISS operation. This last fabrication was eerily similar to the current Russian claim.

This grossly exaggerated story, first published in a supermarket tabloid, was quickly copied to second rate internet web sites. It began to gain traction in mainstream media reporting. This all happened within several weeks of the stories initial release. Like wildfire, it spread globally with more erroneous facts added to its content. Less than two weeks after its initial publication there were more than thirty new stories with varying themes about the rescue and the subsequent Gracian Ultimatum.

Some of these stories also contained comments about what will happen when the deadline does arrive. More than a few talked about how the lack of any action regarding the Ultimatum's demands will bring about the end of the world. These stories made outlandish claims and went into dramatic, exacting, and at times, hysterical detail about how the end of days will occur. They ranged from descriptions of a nuclear holocaust to how the Earth will split apart with thousands of fragments drifting off into space.

Most of the mainstream media tried to legitimize their stories by using actual facts, but they could not resist the temptation to insert opinions and editorial comments of their own choosing. Half-truths and distortions were also inserted as the editors felt they were necessary to make the stories more interesting and more attractive to their audiences.

Television reporting was even worse. Once the nightly and Sunday morning news programs started to do technical interviews, "Experts" began to line up. Some claimed to be knowledgeable about space or the International Space Station, or even extortion situations. Politicians, actors and actresses from film and stage, quickly moved to the front of the line for interviews. Their comments ranged from the absurd to the laughable and for the most part had no basis in fact.

One such actor claimed to be an expert simply because he played in six of the nine Star Wars movies. Another claimed to know about space because he wrote two songs and a poem about it. And finally, there was the politician from California who presented himself as a former NASA employee who had worked a number of years for the space agency. He claimed to have a great deal of firsthand knowledge regarding space and missile launches. After his interview, it was learned that his time with the space agency was actually spent as a cafeteria manager in NASA's Houston facility.

As outlandish as the print, television, and internet reporting was, there was a common conclusion that Planet Grace would not harm or destroy the people of Earth. They went on to believe that the Gracians will issue a second, more serious warning or that they have forgotten about the matter and will simply leave Earth alone.

The stories that did mention annihilation did not get much attention and were not taken seriously. Quite simply, people did not want to hear about threats and destruction. In general, they were naturally optimistic about the situation and just wanted to hear good news.

Throughout the planet, military installations and space agencies had even given up watching for any signs that space vehicles from planet Grace were approaching Earth. Indeed, they felt that Earth was safe.

Chapter 44

Planet Grace Arrives

The two **LRGEVs** have arrived from Planet Grace and are stationed about 550 miles above Earth's North Pole. They are "anchored" about 40 Miles apart and both vehicles are operating in their stealth modes to avoid detection by Earth. They made the 26 light year trip from their planet to Earth in 7 days'. This extraordinarily fast time was made possible by a time-travel like system that was developed by the Gracian's astro-scientists and engineers about 200 years ago. This system has enabled them to greatly expand their galaxy explorations.

The two LRGEV crews have started their bombing preparation work. The first step is to hack into the nuclear control systems of the 10 countries that have nuclear weapons. This has proven to be more difficult owing to security systems enhancements that have been put in place after the Gracian's hacking of 3 years ago.

The Gracian crews are also monitoring military communications, civil broadcasts, and private and public phone conversations in order to get a feel for the current conditions on Earth. So far this effort has yielded no real changs since monitorings three years ago.

Gracian Commander Akar Bou is the onsite person in charge of this mission. Upon arrival in Earth's orbit one of his first duties is to report to the Gracian Space Agency (GSA). His direct report is to agency Director, Ara Quig.

Commander Bou, "Mission Earth 6, mission Earth 6 to GSA come in GSA.

Director Quig, "Mission Earth 6, this is Commander Quig, is that you Akar?

 Commander Bou, "Yes Ara, and this is my initial Earth arrival report. Both LRGEVs are on station, about 550 miles above Earth's North Pole. Our trip was uneventful, and we arrived on time. We have started mission preparations and are having some difficulties with Earth's nuclear control security systems, but it is nothing we can't manage. However, it may slow us down a little. I'll have more on this once we get further along. Otherwise, all else is going well.

Director Quig, "Did you observe any unusual space phenomena during you trip?"

Commander Bou, "Actually, yes we did. **On a journey of this distance,** we, of course, saw the usual meteor sightings, a number of beautiful, far off nebula, some distant planets and moons, and other celestial items. But what really got our attention was a massive explosion event in a far off area, in the direction of the Milky Way's center. This part of Galaxy is known for its activity, and we often see things when passing by this area, but this event was simply tremendous in size. I would guess it was coming from a Supernova. There will probably be a significant debris field emanating from it. We were quite a distance away, far enough to stay out of harm's way, so it was not much of a concern for us. I will send you our estimated coordinates of the area in case you want to investigate it further.

That's all I have for now; I will report again in about 12 hours. Do you have anything else?"

Director Quig, "Yes, Center Director Zon wants to talk to you after you are mission ready, but before you start taking any action towards Earth. You can call me, and I'll connect you to his direct line. He said there is no rush on the call and time of day doesn't matter.

Grace GSA over and out."

Chapter 45

Hazards and Dangers in Space

Space, vast and enigmatic, offers a frontier that has fascinated mankind for centuries. Yet, this seemingly boundless expanse is far from tranquil. From the lethal radiations streaming through the cosmos to the collision risks posed by traveling debris, our universe, the Milky Way, brims with threats that challenge the courage of explorers and the resilience of their spacecrafts. Space Explorers from Earth, Planet Grace and Unknown Planets beyond are all subject to these perils as they venture out into the Great Beyond. This chapter diverts from the book's story and delves into the actual hazards lurking in our celestial realm, including cosmic radiation, space debris, meteors, meteorites, comets, supernovas, and asteroids.

Cosmic Radiation: The Invisible Threat

Cosmic radiation remains one of the most pervasive and dangerous challenges in space. Unlike the radiation we encounter on Earth, which is filtered by our planet's atmosphere and magnetic field, cosmic rays are high-energy particles originating from stars, including our Sun, and celestial events such as supernovas. These rays can penetrate spacecraft, exposing astronauts to increased risks of cancer, tissue damage, and even neurological disorders.

Galactic cosmic rays (GCRs) are particularly potent, comprising nuclei from virtually all elements in the periodic table. Solar particle events (SPEs), associated with solar flares and coronal mass ejections, add to this peril, creating bursts of energetic particles that can overwhelm spacecraft systems. Long-term exposure to these particles necessitates advanced shielding solutions and continuous research to protect human and robotic missions venturing into deep space.

Space Debris: A Growing Menace

As humanity's presence in space increases, so does the accumulation of space debris. Comprised of defunct satellites, discarded rocket stages, and fragments from collisions or explosions, space debris poses a significant hazard. Traveling at speeds exceeding 17,500 miles per hour in low Earth orbit, even a small piece of debris can wreak havoc on active satellites and spacecraft.

The Kessler Syndrome, a theoretical scenario where cascading collisions produce an unmanageable debris field, highlights the dire consequences of unchecked debris proliferation. For astronauts aboard the International Space Station (ISS) and other spacecraft, even the tiniest debris particle could puncture life-support systems. There is a global effort to mitigate this growing risk using debris-tracking programs and initiatives to retrieve or de-orbit defunct objects.

Meteors, Meteorites, and Comets: The Celestial Visitors

Meteors and meteorites, often romanticized as shooting stars or remnants of ancient celestial bodies, carry their own dangers. Meteors are objects from space that burn up upon entering Earth's atmosphere, creating streaks of light. Meteorites, on the other hand, survive their descent and impact Earth's surface. Though most are small, larger meteorites can cause significant damage, such as the Tunguska event in 1908, which flattened thousands of square miles of Siberian forest.

Comets, composed of ice, rock, and dust, orbit the Sun in elongated trajectories. Their tails, formed from sublimated materials driven by solar winds, are breathtaking yet fraught with peril. A collision with Earth by a comet would unleash catastrophic energy, dwarfing nuclear explosions and potentially triggering mass extinctions. While such events are rare, continuous monitoring and advancements in asteroid deflection technologies are crucial to planetary defense.

Supernovas: Cosmic Cataclysms

Few phenomena in the universe rival the sheer power of Supernovas. These stellar explosions occur when stars exhaust their nuclear fuel and collapse under their own gravity or undergo thermonuclear reactions, creating a blast that can outshine entire galaxies. Supernovas release immense amounts of radiation, including gamma rays, capable of sterilizing nearby planets and disrupting entire ecosystems.

While Earth lies relatively safe from direct supernova threats due to the vast distances separating us from the nearest candidates, such explosions remind us of the volatile nature of the cosmos. Scientists study supernovas to understand their impact on planetary systems and gauge the risks posed by nearby stars nearing the end of their life cycles.

Asteroids: The Persistent Threat

Asteroids, rocky fragments left over from the formation of solar systems and other cosmic explosions, represent a persistent danger to space explorers. Our galaxy actually has an Asteroid Belt which contains millions of asteroids. It is located between Mars and Jupiter. On occasion asteroids will leave the belt and stray into paths or orbits that bring them perilously close to habitable planets. On Earth they are known as Near-Earth Objects (NEOs), these asteroids are tracked meticulously by international space agencies.

The Chicxulub asteroid, which struck Earth 66 million years ago and contributed to the extinction of the dinosaurs, underscores the catastrophic potential of asteroid impacts. Efforts to mitigate such risks include initiatives like NASA's DART (Double Asteroid Redirection Test) mission, which aims to deflect asteroids using kinetic impact techniques. These strategies highlight humanity's proactive approach to guarding against asteroid threats.

The Interconnected Nature of Space Hazards

While each hazard in space presents unique challenges, their interconnected nature complicates mitigation efforts.

For instance, cosmic radiation can exacerbate electronic malfunctions in spacecraft causing them to collide with space debris. Similarly, the aftermath of asteroid or comet impacts might generate additional debris, compounding threats to orbiting satellites and space missions.

Space exploration, though fraught with hazards, embodies humanity's indomitable spirit of discovery and innovation. The dangers posed by cosmic radiation, space debris, meteors, meteorites, comets, supernovas, and asteroids are stark reminders of the universe's unpredictability and power. Yet, through advancements in technology, international collaboration, and a deep commitment to understanding the cosmos, we continue to push boundaries and extend our reach into the stars. These efforts not only redefine our place in the universe but also ensure the safety and sustainability of our ventures beyond Earth's protective embrace.

Chapter 46

"A Day" Is Almost Here

The Grace Ultimatum (annihilation) date or "A Day" as the media is calling it is now ten days away. Up until a month ago the majority of Earth's citizenry felt that they were safe from the threat of the Gracian Ultimatum. Some even thought that the aliens had forgotten about it and would leave Earth alone. The few articles and editorials that were written about the date were relegated to the back pages newspapers and periodicals.

However, the recent increase of Ultimatum reporting is having a major effect on world populations. The almost daily barrage of exaggerated or distorted news reporting has eroded optimism towards Earth's safety. People are now starting to worry about their own wellbeing and the media is now using words like apocalyptic, Armageddon and even Judgement day to describe possible coming events.

This reporting has also created a new wave of anger and discontent towards governments, and public officials due to their lack of action. Mass protests are being held in major cities and rioting and looting is starting to occur. Politicians are running for safety and cover. Civility and sanity are being abandoned in favor of mob rule.

Powerful voices are being raised to quell the discontent, and they are asking for peace and calm. They are also attempting to point out the obvious that the threat to their planet and themselves is coming from a source outside of Earth's control and there is nothing much that can be done about it except wait and hope that the Gracians show mercy or tolerance. But this message is almost impossible to get across as few want to hear it.

The Media is mostly to blame for creating this situation; however, they do not see it that way. They say that it is their job to report the news no matter how good or how bad it is. Further, they claim to have done their job well, and they bear no responsibility for actions taken by the public based on the facts as reported by them. Lacking accountability, what they fail to mention is how truth and accuracy were skewed in order to enliven their stories to attract readers.

Out in space and high above the North Pole, the Gracians are monitoring the chaotic situation on earth, and they are appalled by what they see. Three years ago, a Gracians representative delivered an ultimatum to the people of Earth. At first the terms were greeted with enthusiasm and even applauded with Earthlings agreeing that certain conditions had to change in order to make the planet a better place to live. Then almost three years later and with the deadline looming, no meaningful changes have been made, and the people of Earth are starting to riot against their own leaders for lack of action.

The Gracians do not know quite what to make of this behavior. But they do agree that Earth is indeed a strange planet and one that they would not want to inhabit.

Commander Bou has sent an informational report on these current observations to the Center back on planet Grace.

In the meantime, plant Grace's LRGEV crews are continuing their work on gaining access to Earth's nuclear weapon control centers and they are making steady progress.

Chapter 47

One Week to Go

It is now seven days before "A Day" and two major factions have emerged from the Grace Ultimatum issue.

One group is made up of "believers", people or countries who believe that something will happen on the Ultimatum due date. They are not sure what, but their concerns and fears range from an extension of the date to the detonation of more nuclear bombs. None of these people believe that Earth will be totally destroyed. They generally live in the Western Hemisphere and parts of Europe and Africa. They make up approximately 36% of the world population. This area is seeing most of the demonstrations, riots and civil disobedience.

The other large group is made up of "non-believers". For the most part, they never thought that the Ultimatum was real and believed that the U.N. address was staged by some western faction and that the so called spaceship was a product of Hollywood. The fact that no one has heard from the Gracians over the past three years further strengthens their position. Since the beginning, their governments have fostered the non-belief theory among their citizenry and together with their blind obedience towards their rulers has gone a long way towards convincing the undecided to join in their thinking. They inhabit various parts of the Eastern Hemisphere and make up approximately 47% of the world population.

The balance of people in the world, some 17% are indifferent or not even aware of the Gracian situation although with all of the recent news coverage they are beginning to hear about it.

Surprisingly, science and religion have not played much of a role in whether or not people believe in the deadline and its ultimatum.

In the meantime, Gracian crews aboard the two **LRGEVs** have gained access to Earth's Nuclear weapon control systems and have completed all of their mission preparations. They are currently in a "ready" mode and are awaiting orders to proceed

Chapter 48

The Go Ahead Call

Commander Bou is preparing to call the Center's lead Director, Zon to obtain final approval to commence the mission to destroy Earth. The discussions and soul searching are over and all that remains is to get the job done. He was alone with his thoughts when the LRGEVs command center advised him that a call was coming through from Director Zon.

Director Zon, "Come in Commander Bou".

"This is commander Bou. Director Zon, I was just about to call you. We are ready to proceed with the mission, and I wanted to obtain final approval before proceeding".

Director Zon, "Something has come up and I am going to ask you to hold off starting the mission. Let me explain the circumstances.

We followed up on your report of the massive event, or explosion as you called it, in the direction of the Milky Way's Center. We have determined that the event actually took place just inside the fringes of our galaxy. It was so large that from your point of view it may have appeared to be coming from the galaxy's center. We determined it was, in fact, the action of a Supernova, but we have no idea of its origin. We don't even know if it occurred within the bounds of our Milky Way Galaxy or if it wandered in from another part of what the Earthlings call the Local Void.

"Director, can you fill me in on this Local Void business? What is it?

"The Local Void which the Earthlings discovered around 1987, is a vast area in space which includes the Milky Way the galaxy we share with Earth, Andromeda our closest neighboring galaxy, a number of other galaxies and some sundry cosmic items. It is enormous, possibly 150 million light years across, but determining its size is tricky because of its amorphous shape"

"Director, I take it that this is not what the Earthling's call a Black Hole."

"No commander, a Black Hole is an astronomical object with a gravitational pull so strong that nothing, not even light, can escape it. This is because the "surface" of a black hole, called the event horizon, defines the boundary where the escape velocity actually exceeds the speed of light.

By contrast the Local Void simply describes an area in space and includes an inventory of items that are contained within it."

Director Zon, "Getting back to my call, the force of the event you witnessed was so powerful that we expect it to launch sizeable pieces of debris far and wide across the galaxy at speeds up to hundreds of thousands of miles per hour. Some of the debris pieces could be quite large, perhaps as big as a small moon or planet. Fortunately, our planet, Grace, does not appear to be in the debris path, but I can't say the same for Earth. That planet does fall within the estimated debris zone and due to the almost hyper speed of the debris, Earth could start to feel it's effects in as little as seven to ten days. We have dispatched an unmanned space prob to gather more information about the debris field and we will know more in a day or so.

The reason we are putting the mission on hold is that this cosmic anomaly may very well solve our problem with Earth."

"Director, are you saying that a large enough piece of debris originating from this event could be enough to destroy Planet Earth?

"Exactly, and if it doesn't then we can proceed with our mission. In the meantime, I am asking you to stand down, remain in place, and await further orders."

Commander Bou, "Yes sir, we will stand-by and await further orders. Mission Earth 6, over and out"

The next day, Planet Grace's Space Command advises Commander Bou that data from the space probe does in fact confirm that debris created by the Supernova event is headed towards the area of Earth and its moon. As a consequence, both Commanders were advised that the mission will remain on hold and they should leave their location as soon as possible and seek shelter on the far side of Plant Mars, some 140 million miles away.

Chapter 49

Peek–A-Boo

It is now six days before "A Day". The status quo on Earth has not changed. Some groups are continuing with their demonstrations while others are going about their business as usual with nary a thought about Planet Grace, their Ultimatum, or anything else that may interrupt their daily routines.

The 73rd Space Group was established on January 1,1967. It is located at Falcon Air Force Base near Colorado Springs, Colorado. The group is responsible for surveilling, detecting, tracking, and reporting unusual space objects. They do this by operating various sensors, electro-optical surveillance systems, mechanical and phased array radars, and passive radio frequency detection systems. Surveillance data is transferred to the group's Command and Control Headquarters located at the Cheyenne Mountain Air Force Base at Colorado Springs. The command and control group utilize this data to maintain a comprehensive catalog of all artificial objects in orbit. Tracking data is also transmitted to the North American Aerospace Defense Command,(NORAD), the U.S. Space Command and a network of member space observer groups located throughout the world.

The 73rd group were the first to detect the departure of Grace's two LRGEVs from their position, 500 miles above the North Pole. Before this detection, the 73rd group or anyone else for that matter, were aware of the LRGEV 's presence. Given the current hype and media attention of anything Gracian, this detection was immediately reported to the uppermost command of the military and on to the White House.

 The questions came quickly; How long were they here? What were they doing? Did they make contact with anyone? and Where did they go? Unfortunately, these questions could only be met with conjecture as no one knew the answers

The White House made one thing very clear and that was that this detection had to be classified and handled as "Top Secret" because any news of this sighting could create worldwide chaos. Unfortunately, the secrecy could not be maintained. Two observatories and the observation group of the European Space Agency also witnessed the movement away from Earth of the two LRGEV's. They also had questions. Chief among them were, Why were they here? and Why did they leave?

News of the LRGEVs soon leaked to the media which immediately spread it globally. With no official comments from the authorities, the media was left to their own devices to report on what the leaker or leakers had to say. In most cases the reporting included speculation, guesses, and of course outright fake news. This gave rise to more civil unrest, riots and even an uptick in the number of suicides. Even the non-believers began to sit up and take notice. The latest news reporting became a catalyst pushing civil disorder to the brink with some very bad things starting to happen.

Power outages were starting because power station operators and maintenance personal were walking off the job or just not showing up for work. The public transportation sector was having difficulties maintaining schedules due to locomotive engineers, bus drivers and even airline pilots not showing up for work. Transportation disruptions were starting to have an effect on goods, services and food availability. Hording became prevalent and looting was occurring.

To their credit, local, state and federal law enforcement workers were doing their best to maintain some semblance of order. Many churches, synagogues, mosques, temples and tabernacles were full of people seeking divine intervention for the current disorder.

This disorder happened in a very short space of time.

Chapter 50

"A" Day And The Morning After

"A" Day, has arrived on Earth. To believers the waiting has been excruciating, and the anxiety is palatable. Worker absenteeism has skyrocketed, and nothing seems to be getting done. People just seemed to be waiting but most do not know exactly what they are waiting for. Power interruptions are frequently occurring and meany areas are without electricity. Public transportation has ceased, and grocery store shelves are all but empty. And everyone continues to wait.

In areas where non-believers prevail, things are quite normal. The only real disruptions are those caused by interactions with the believer areas.

It is now three days since "A" Day has past, and there has been no action or events tied to the Gracian Ultimatum and everyone one is taking credit for it. The non-believers are saying "we told you so" and "it's like Y2K all over again". The religious folks are saying that their prayers were answered and that God did intervene. The folks that seemed to be indifferent about the whole Gracian matter are just happy that things are getting back to normal

Normalcy is indeed starting to return to plant Earth and in the absence of any real Gracian threat, lessons learned from this calamity will be quickly put aside and forgotten.

The feeling among the NASA folks and others directly involved in the actual space station rescue see it differently. They had direct contact with some of the Gracian **LRGEV** personal and their collective opinion was that the Gracian's are honest and sincere people who meant what they said. The NASA folks and their compatriots are genuinely puzzled as to why there has not been action or at least some type of communication from the Gracians.

Chapter 51

Just When You Thought It Was Safe

The surveillance team of the 73rd Space Group were the first to identify an object resembling a large meteor, surrounded by a significant cloud of dust and gas. It was initially detected in a remote section of the Milky Way, moving at high speed towards the general direction of Earth. At this point, Its distance, size, speed, and path could not be accurately determined. The object's velocity has alarmed observers, who had not previously recorded such speed in their observations of other space objects. They immediately reported the sighting to their high command, classified it as "Top Secret", and put their base on "High Alert".

This classification and alerting immediately set off a chain of events that went all the way to the White House. As the object continued on its course, the space group was able to gather more precise information. Their recent calculations put the path of the object as passing through an oval shaped area which included the Planets, Mars and Earth including its moon.

United States President, Frank Hays has called an emergency cabinet meeting to review the matter.

President Hays, "This is the second time in 10 days that we are meeting to discuss some external force that is threating our planet and by consequence, our country so this better not be another false alarm!"

Secretary of Defense Meyers, "Sir, I can assure you that this object is real and it is on a path that has it passing through our area of the galaxy. At this point we cannot say with any certainty whether or not it will hit us."

"What else do we know, will it take out Mars? Will it hit our Moon and if so what are the consequences? How big is it? How close to Earth does it have to come to give us problems? Can we shoot it down?

Secretary of Defense Meyers," This object is very large, about the size if Bermuda. It is travelling hundreds of thousands of miles per hour. If it were to hit Mars it would cause a great deal of surface destruction but not much else because we know of no life on that planet. There is the possibility that the impact could cause the planet to break apart, but we just don't know

President Hays, "What if it hits Earth?"

Secretary of Defense Meyers, "That is another story and a far more consequential and devastating one.

The largest known asteroid to hit Earth was about 66 million years ago. It was about 6 – 9 miles wide and hit an area around the Yucatan Peninsula leaving behind the massive Chicxulub crater. It also triggered the Cretaceous–Paleogene mass extinction event that wiped out 75% of living plant and animal species including the dinosaurs.

Given the size of this asteroid, if it were to hit Earth the energy force released from the impact would be the equivalent of thousands of nuclear bombs. It would immediately wipe out all forms of human, animal, and plant life. Our planet would be reduced to a dark, lifeless remnant that would ultimately vanish into the void of space."

President Hays, "Can we shoot it down?

Secretary of Defense Meyers, "Again given the size of the object I do not believe a nuclear bomb, or a series of nuclear bombs would have much of an impact."

President Hays, "Can't we just fire off a couple of hundred ICBMs with nuclear war heads and blast it into pieces? Even if some pieces got through, it would be better than having the whole thing hit us! How much time do we have before this thing hits us?

Secretary of Defense Meyers, "We have not looked into the use of nuclear weapons as a deterrent.

If all conditions remain as they are now, we estimate impact would occur in about 96 hours. But we still do not know for certain where or what it will impact in the projected strike zone."

President Hays, "Mr. Meyers we are quite possibly facing a doomsday situation. We must think outside the box. For starters I want you to come up with a plan to fire as many nuclear bombs as possible at this thing, and I would like to hear of any other solutions from your boys at the Pentagon may have. You have six hours to report back to me. Oh, and one other thing I would like updates every two hours on the speed, position and course of this object."

Secretary of Defense Meyers, "Yes Sir"

President Hays, "Secretary of State Rodriguez, I would like you to come up with a communication plan and your advice on which heads of state I should be talking to about this and what we should be saying.

Chief of Staff Wilson, please get with the press secretary and develop a press release outline.

Does anyone else have anything to add, any questions?

Yes, Secretary of Agriculture, Benson."

"Sir, If impact becomes inevitable, and we run out of options, have you thought about what you, your family and the rest of our country will do?"

President Hays, "Yes, I have given it some thought. I will definitely address the nation when the time comes, however for the time being, I will keep to myself what I will say and do. If there no other questions I will adjourn the meeting. Meeting adjourned"

Eighteen hours have passed since the President's meeting. There has been no change in the object's general trajectory and calculations continue to show that a collision with Earth is becoming more likely. Recently, it has been noted that the object is moving in a slight zigzag path instead of a straight line. This motion may have been there all along and not noticed due to distance. It is not known if this will affect its future path towards Earth.

The American military has developed a plan to fire a huge salvo of nuclear armed missiles at the object as it nears Earth. The United States has enlisted the aid of Great Britian and Israel to add to the missile salvo. France and China have agreed to act as a backups.

In addition, the United States has relayed current information about the object and the mitigation plan to a number of other countries.

An official White House statement has not yet been issued out of concerns about starting a worldwide panic. However, thanks to leaks, the media has a fairly good idea of what is going on. Most have released their own versions of the story and some are amazingly accurate.

The White House feels that these stories may actually soften the blow, so to speak when the official account of events is released to the public.

Even without the release of an official notification from world leaders, a majority of the world population knows what may be in store for them and their behavior remains quite civil, almost apathetic. Some riots are continuing, although to what end it is not very clear, "no shows" at work are on the rise and the resulting slowdown of vital services is starting to show. Generally, there is an uneasy calm about the world. Churches and other religious institution are being overwhelmed with worshipers, but calm and camaraderie appears to be the order of the day.

It was evident that once again people found themselves waiting for something to happen, but most were hoping that it would not.

It is now 72 hours before the estimated collision time between Earth and the android. Nothing much has changed, and it is still on a zigzag pattern, however this variance is not enough to avoid colliding with Earth and conditions on the planet remain stable.

Chapter 52

Rumblings

There are a number of agencies that monitor and research Earthquakes. They are primarily run by governments or academic research centers. Many of them are located in earthquake "hot spots" throughout the world. For the most part their mission statements are all very similar.

"Determine the location and size of all significant earthquakes worldwide, disseminate the information immediately to all partners, maintain an online database of the seismic events, and perform earthquake research."

About 10 days before the estimated asteroid collision date, scientist at the California Institute of Technology (Cal Tech), Pasadena noticed that an unusual number of earth tremors we occurring in various places throughout the world. Adding to this anomaly was that they were occurring at the same time. They we not considered significant as most were in a Richter Scale range of 2.5 to 3.0 and not very noticeable.

Thanks to the immediate dissemination procedures, the Caltech data was quickly picked up by worldwide earthquake monitoring groups. Their consensus was that the quake frequencies were unusual but given their minor scale, were not anything to be concerned about. Besides at this point, most scientist were focused on the approaching asteroid.

About 3 days later another, simultaneous tremor event occurred. This time the tremors were slightly stronger, in the 2.5 to 3.4 Richter Scale range and they were now being referred to as earthquakes, not tremors.

The question that was on the mind of the earthquake watchers was, could the tremor events be somehow tied to the approaching android?

One earthquake scientist was significantly more concerned. His name was Sir Augustus Ross or Gus, as he is known. Sir Gus was born in Kirkwall, in the Orkney Isles of Scotland. He was a bright lad who was fascinated by things that made the earth move beneath his feet including Earthquakes. He attend Eaton, MIT and then Cal Tech where he studied Geology and earned a PhD in Seismology. He was knighted by Queen Elizabeth for his work in the field of early earthquake detection.

Sir Gus has been working on a theory that addresses the overloading of the Earth's natural venting system caused by the extraction of Hydrocarbons, i.e. Crude Oil and Natural Gas from the Earth's crust over the past century

To understand Gus' theory and how it may explain the recently reported rumblings it may be helpful to review a little about Earth itself.

Scientist estimate that the Earth has been around for 4.5 billion years. It originated from a massive dust and gas cloud known as a solar nebula. This cloud collapsed under its own gravity, with a sun forming at its center. The remaining material flattened into a spinning disk, a process known as accretion. Over Billions of years mountains deserts, oceans, and many other features coalesced to become the planet we know as Earth.

The planet itself is made up of three major sections:

- **Crust** The Earth's covering with an average thickness of 9 to 12 miles depending mountain heights and ocean depths. The deepest recording drilling into the crust is approximately 9 miles. This is the deepest man has penetrated the Earth.
- **Mantle** This section comprises approximately 80% of the planet's volume. Temperatures in the mantle range from about 1,800°F near the Crust boundary to 6,700°F adjacent to the Core. The mantle is composed of solid rock consisting of metals and other elements. It does exhibit some plasticity at tectonic plate boundaries and mantle plumes. It approaches a nearly liquid state close to the Core boundary.

- **<u>Core</u>**

   The Core is the innermost section of the planet. It consists of two parts. The Outer Core lies beneath the mantel. It is a hot, a 9,000°F liquid mass consisting of iron and nickel. It is about 1,400 miles thick.

   The Inner Core lies at the center of the Earth. It is made up of a solid mass of an iron-nickel alloy and is about two-thirds the size of Earth's moon. The inner core is very hot, 10,000 °F which about the surface temperature of the Sun.

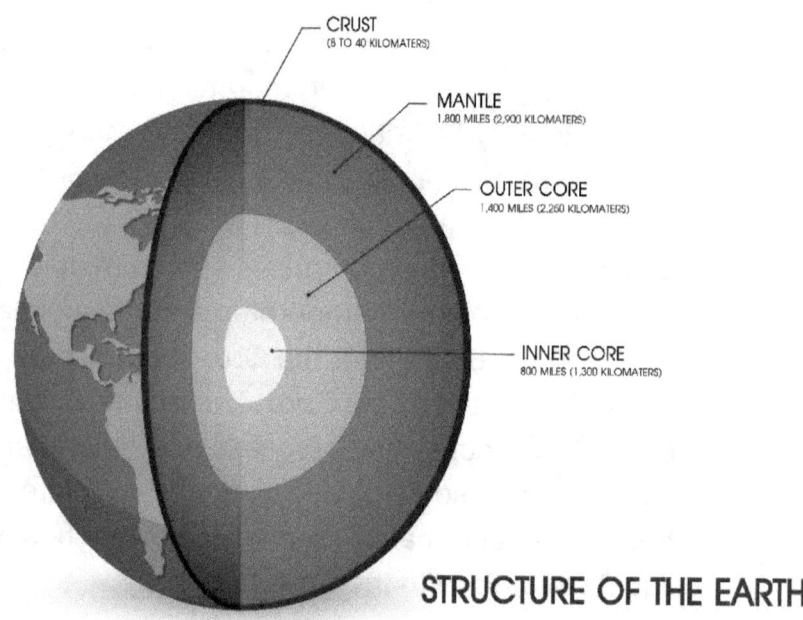

STRUCTURE OF THE EARTH

Below its Crust, the Earth is a hot place. On occasion subterranean activity creates additional heat which vents through fissures and through the more than 1,500 volcanos that populate the Earth. Sir Gus refers to this as the Earth's natural venting system.

His research focuses on the affect oil well drilling has had on the Earth's Crust and any harm it may have caused to the natural venting system.

Early man first noticed crude oil as it oozed from seeps in the Earth's Crust. Initially this sticky, gooey material had no use. However, it was eventually used in medicines, as a waterproofing material for boats and for lighting (torches). Archives in China, circa 600 BC, show oil being moved from place to place using bamboo pipes. In 1875, Crude Oil was discovered in Pennsylvania and ushered in the development of a major energy industry.

By 2025, it is estimated that 1.6 trillion barrels of oil will have been extracted from oil-bearing sands and reservoirs within the Earth's Crust. In light of this substantial volume removal, Sir Gus is investigating whether this extraction has resulted in voids that may compromise the structural integrity of the Crust and its natural venting systems.

Recently he has stumbled upon a discovery indicating that voids created by oil and gas removal may be filling with water from the world's oceans. Sir Gus does not see this as a problem by itself. However, if the sea water finds its way down to the Mantel's heat it will immediately turn into superheated steam and create massive explosions that would overload the Earth's venting system and cause fractures in the planet and even worse could even blow the planet apart. Sir Gus does not have enough empirical evidence to prove this will happen, but he does feel the rumblings may definitely be a harbinger of things that will soon occur.

OIL WELL STRUCTURE

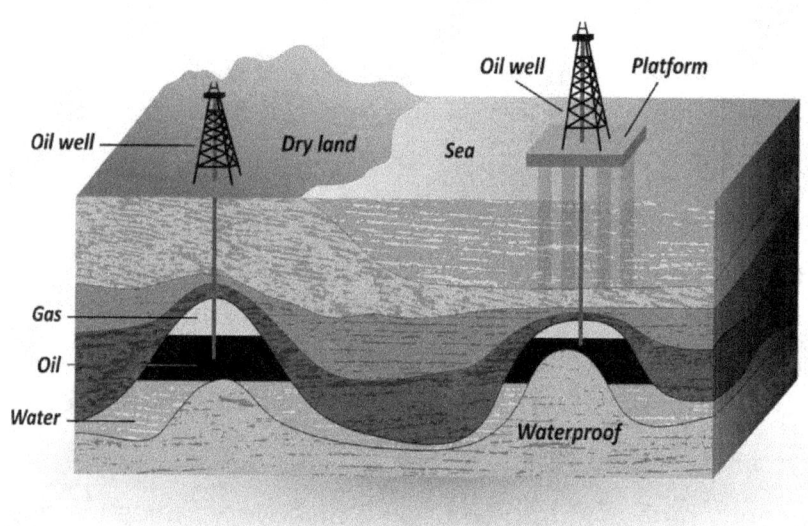

Chapter 53

Armageddon

The time before contact between the asteroid and Earth is about 24 hours. The asteroid's slightly zig zag course has not changed nor has its speed which places its current location about 11 million miles from Earth and closing fast.

Calm conditions prevail on the doomed planet. Riots and looting have all but ceased, very few planes are flying, trains are no longer running, and less than half of the planet has electricity. Religious facilities continue to draw huge crowds and the critically ill are dying at a faster rate due to the lack of medical personnel reporting for work. Remarkably, cell phones continue to work as long as batteries hold out.

Thanks to spares, back-ups and emergency equipment, the military along with some police organizations are still operating at a fairly high capacity.

Most people on Earth have accepted the asteroid threat as unavoidable, and believe escape is impossible. However, some have chosen to take control over how their life will end rather than wait passively for the inevitable.

A renewed sense of optimism has emerged among asteroid observers at Cal Tech. The asteroid in question is currently passing planet Jupiter, a gas giant possessing a mass 2.5 times that of Earth. Jupiter's gravitational field, 2.4 times stronger than Earth's, appears to be influencing the asteroid's trajectory and velocity. Rather than following its earlier zigzag path, the asteroid is now exhibiting a more stable course with a minor deviation of approximately one degree to the right. Although this adjustment is relatively slight, considering the vast distance to Earth, it could result in the asteroid missing the planet by several hundred thousand miles.

The Cal Tech scientists are not yet in a position to disclose their findings to the public as more details are needed. In addition, they want to see if a more favorable movement occurs as the asteroid careens towards Earth. So, for right now, they are taking a wait-and-see position.

Eight hours have passed, and the one degree course deviation has increased another half a degree, and the scientists have observed a slight reduction in speed. Still more time is needed before any reporting takes place.

In the meantime, conditions on Earth remain unchanged.

Chapter 54

All Clear

The asteroids course deviation is holding steady, and Cal Tech's assessment that it will miss Earth has been confirmed by other scientists. The public has been informed, and life is returning to normal. The world is taking a collective sigh of relief.

Upon hearing the news, the Gracian high command has given the order to resume their mission to destroy Earth. The fact the Earth was spared destruction by the asteroid collision only means that they will have to finish the job. Gracian Space Command has ordered their two spacecraft to return to their previous location above Earth and await further orders. A short time later the spacecraft arrive on station and report that they are ready to resume the mission.

The prevailing euphoria on Earth has temporarily diverted the attention of most people from the uptick in seismological activity. Sir Augustus Ross, however, remains acutely aware of the situation. He is deeply concerned. His sensors and instruments are indicating that significant low level earthquakes are occurring simultaneously across the globe with little respite, and their intensity is on the rise.

Sir Ross is in a quandary as to what action he should take. Reporting the quake activity to his fellow scientist would get some understanding of the situation but not much action would be forthcoming. Reporting it to governing authorities could get some action but even if they believed the threat was real, what could they do? What could anyone do for that matter?

As he is sitting in his office pondering this dilemma, he notices that his sensors and monitors have become more active. An exceptionally large 8.2 earthquake has just occurred in the Atlantic Ocean just off the coast of Iceland and another in Reyad, Saudi Arabia. Minutes later another quake occurs in the Marianas Trench in the South Pacific. Soon after, very strong eruptions hit the Mauna Lea, and Kilauea volcanoes, in Hawaii. Another strong quake is detected in the Java Trench. All of the quakes register 9+ on the Richter scale and are creating tsunamis with significant wave heights. During the next half hour, five more 9+ quakes are detected, and 3 dormant volcanoes experience extraordinarily strong eruptions.

Sir Ross realizes that his theory is becoming a reality.

News of these quakes is not being widely broadcast due to the pre-asteroid work no-shows which had shut down a number of global communication networks. However, people in the quake areas are most certainly aware of them.

The recent rise in seismic activity, along with the associated extreme pressure forces, is leading to an increased number of fractures or fissures in the Earth's crust. These newly formed pathways are allowing greater volumes of ocean water to contact the heat of the Mantle. This water contact is producing enormous amounts of superheated steam (steam occupies approximately 1,000 times more space than water). This expansion is exerting additional pressure on the Earth's crust. Sir Ross has no idea what effect it may be having on the Earth's Mantle and Core or even if the planet can survive this onslaught.

This geographic phenomena is getting progressively worse. More volcanos are erupting, earthquakes, now 10+ on the Richter Scale, are occurring with greater frequency, tsunamis are becoming more devastating, and ocean levels are actually starting to drop as they flood towards Earth's inner core. All of this is happening in a short space of time and the people of Earth have not even had a chance to react to it.

Those who have survived so far are literally in shock. Buildings, bridges, and other structures are collapsing or just toppling over, dams are bursting, and a number of nuclear weapons have detonated. Almost as quickly as this upheaval of earth started, a scant 6 hours ago, a cessation of activity occurs. Earth, the "Big Blue Marble" it once was has been reduced to a dismal gray sphere covered by volcanic ash laden clouds, large swatches of fires, and muddy discolored oceans. But a certain calm and quite has settled upon the planet.

The calm is not long lasting. About one hour later a tremendous explosion occurs the likes of which have never been seen or heard before on Earth. It started in the Aleutian Trench and traveled down the Eurasian "Ring of Fire" trenches, coming to a stop at New Zealand.

This blast literally opened up the Earth right down to its inner Core releasing Mantel and Core material up to 10,000° F. This flash of heat incinerated every remaining living thing on planet Earth. The force was so great it caused the Earth to fall out of orbit and break apart sending thousands of pieces, some measuring hundreds of square miles, into the vast reaches of space. These pieces will eventually break apart and join the billions of other unnamed objects that populate the Milky Way and beyond.

Planet Earth no longer exists.

Chapter 55

Aftermath

Plant Grace's two **LRGEVs** are on their way home. They were lucky to escape the seismic calamity of Earth's destruction. Commander Bou is personally relieved that he did not have to carry out his mission. His past contact and even friendship with some of the Earthlings added a personal element to the task, one which the leaders of Planet Grace were lacking. In addition, he was more in favor of the Wait-and-See Monitoring Plan as it still gave the Earthlings more time to correct their ways.

All of this does not matter of course because in the end, unbeknownst to the Earthlings, they destroyed their own planet. It took them over one hundred years of oil well drilling to do it, but they did it.

Three years later, Planet Grace was completely destroyed by the same asteroid that threatened Earth.

THE END

RESCUE

www.ingramcontent.com/pod-product-compliance
Lightning Source LLC
Chambersburg PA
CBHW062129170626
46813CB00002B/624

* 9 7 9 8 9 9 1 1 7 1 5 2 6 *